A Halloween Love Story

Sarah Baker

Published by Bright Minds Books, 2024.

This is a work of fiction. Similarities to real people, places, or events are entirely coincidental.

A HALLOWEEN LOVE STORY

First edition. October 9, 2024.

Copyright © 2024 Sarah Baker.

ISBN: 979-8227839817

Written by Sarah Baker.

Table of Contents

Chapter 1: The First Encounter 1
Chapter 2: A Hauntingly Good Start 5
Chapter 3: The Halloween Decoration Hunt 9
Chapter 4: The Pumpkin Patch Date 13
Chapter 5: Spooky Movie Marathon 17
Chapter 6: Haunted Hayride 22
Chapter 7: The Halloween Costume Decision 27
Chapter 8: The Halloween Party 31
Chapter 9: Trick-or-Treat for Adults 36
Chapter 10: Visiting a Real Haunted House 41
Chapter 11: The Halloween Bakery 46
Chapter 12: The Ghost Tour 51
Chapter 13: The Costume Competition 56
Chapter 14: The Pumpkin Carving Contest 60
Chapter 15: The Halloween Maze Adventure 65
Chapter 16: The Midnight Cemetery Visit 70
Chapter 17: Halloween Traditions Revealed 75
Chapter 18: The Fortune Teller's Prediction 79
Chapter 19: Halloween at Home 83
Chapter 20: The Night of the Masquerade Ball 87
Chapter 21: The Unexpected Twist 91
Chapter 22: Halloween Morning Fun 96
Chapter 23: Halloween Proposal 100
Chapter 24: A Halloween Wedding Dream 104
Chapter 25: The Relationship Vow 108

Description

When Tom and Ella bump into each other while shopping for Halloween decorations, their worlds change forever.

What begins as a chance encounter blossoms into a whirlwind of Halloween-themed adventures—haunted houses, pumpkin carving contests, ghost tours, and more. As their connection deepens, they discover that their love is just as magical as the season. From costume competitions to midnight cemetery visits, their relationship grows through each spooky celebration.

In this charming love story, Halloween becomes the backdrop for an unexpected romance, leading to a heartwarming vow to spend the rest of their lives together.

Dedication

To those who find magic in the small moments and believe that love, like Halloween, can be full of surprises. This story is for those who embrace the thrill of life's adventures, and for the ones who make every season unforgettable.

And to the memory of fall evenings, pumpkin-flavored everything, and the joy of being with someone who feels like home.

Preface

Halloween has always been a time of transformation—a season where the ordinary becomes extraordinary, and where the unexpected can happen.

When I first thought about writing a love story set against the backdrop of Halloween, I knew it had to capture more than just the fun and thrills of the season. It had to be about connection, about the magic that happens when two people's lives intertwine in the most unexpected ways.

This story is a celebration of that magic—a tale of Tom and Ella, who discover that sometimes, love arrives when you least expect it, and in the most unlikely places. It's a reminder that love, like Halloween, can be both thrilling and full of warmth.

Chapter 1: The First Encounter

Tom adjusted his scarf, feeling the cool October breeze nip at his skin. He loved everything about fall: the crisp air, the fiery-colored leaves, and most of all, Halloween. Today was the day he'd been waiting for all year. He'd cleared his schedule to visit one of his favorite spots in town—a local Halloween shop renowned for its elaborate decorations and vast selection of spooky treasures.

As he entered the store, the comforting scent of cinnamon and cloves wafted toward him, blending with the artificial fog from a nearby smoke machine. Orange and black streamers hung from the ceiling, creating a festive atmosphere, while eerie music played softly in the background. Tom immediately felt at home among the rows of ghostly decorations, jack-o'-lanterns, and racks of costumes.

He grabbed a basket and began perusing the aisles. After living in his apartment for nearly three years, this would be his first Halloween where he'd actually go all out on decorations. There were skeletons that danced, tombstones that glowed, and animatronic witches cackling in the corners. Every item tempted him, but he was determined to stick to a theme this year—classic horror with a twist of humor.

As he wandered into the aisle dedicated to pumpkins, he spotted the perfect jack-o'-lantern. Its grinning face, lit from within by flickering LED lights, reminded him of the ones he used to carve with his family when he was younger. Without hesitation, he reached out to grab it.

At the same exact moment, another hand brushed against his.

Startled, Tom quickly pulled back and turned toward the owner of the other hand. His gaze fell upon a woman who looked just as surprised as he was. Her warm brown eyes sparkled under the store's dim lighting, and a strand of dark hair fell from her knit cap, framing her face. She looked at him, eyes wide with a mixture of shock and amusement.

"Oh! I'm sorry," she laughed softly, her voice warm and inviting. "Didn't mean to steal your pumpkin."

Tom grinned. "No worries. Looks like we've got good taste in Halloween décor."

She smiled, releasing the jack-o'-lantern and allowing Tom to pick it up. "Apparently so. I was just thinking it would make the perfect centerpiece for my apartment."

Tom tilted his head, intrigued. "Halloween fan?"

"Absolutely. It's my favorite holiday. I've been decorating since I was a kid," she said, tucking a loose strand of hair behind her ear. "I'm Ella, by the way."

"Tom," he replied, shifting the pumpkin under his arm and extending his free hand. They shook hands, and Tom felt an unexpected spark of excitement. Maybe it was the season, or maybe it was the way her smile lit up her face, but there was something about her that made him want to keep talking.

"Nice to meet you, Tom." Ella glanced down at the pumpkin again, then back up at him. "So, do you always shop for Halloween decorations at the last minute, or is this a one-time thing?"

Tom chuckled. "Usually, I'm more organized, but this year I'm going all out. I'm finally setting up my apartment like one of those haunted houses you see in magazines."

Ella's eyes lit up with interest. "That sounds amazing. I'm doing something similar, but I'm more into quirky decorations—like zombie garden gnomes or vampire bats that sing."

Tom laughed, imagining her apartment filled with whimsical Halloween decor. "Sounds like we're going for completely opposite vibes, but both sound fun."

She nodded in agreement. "Definitely. I've always loved the fun side of Halloween, but I can appreciate a good haunted house. Do you build your own haunted mazes, too?"

"I haven't yet, but that's a solid idea. Maybe I'll try something like that next year," Tom said, already imagining turning his small living room into a maze of cobwebs and flickering lights.

For a moment, they stood in comfortable silence, surrounded by the bustling shoppers and festive chaos of the store. Ella glanced at the other decorations, her hand lightly brushing a witch's broomstick hanging nearby.

"I was actually planning to decorate this weekend," Ella said, her tone casual but hopeful. "If you need any ideas or help, I'm pretty good at setting the spooky mood."

Tom raised an eyebrow, a grin forming on his lips. "Are you offering to be my Halloween consultant?"

"Only if you need one," she teased, her eyes twinkling mischievously. "But fair warning, I take Halloween very seriously."

"Sounds like a challenge," Tom said, matching her playful tone. "I might take you up on that. What do you say we compare notes on decorations? Maybe grab a coffee afterward?"

Ella hesitated for a brief moment, her smile widening. "I'd like that."

They exchanged phone numbers, and as Tom added her contact to his phone, he felt a surge of excitement that had nothing to do with Halloween decorations. There was something easy about talking to her, like they'd known each other longer than the few minutes they'd spent together in the store.

"So," Ella said, glancing down at her basket filled with cobwebs and plastic spiders, "any other must-haves on your shopping list?"

"Definitely need some more creepy lighting," Tom said, scanning the nearby shelves. "And maybe a few more skulls. Can never have too many skulls."

Ella laughed, her laughter bright and contagious. "Agreed. I'm here for the fake blood and fog machines."

"Going all out with the effects, huh?"

"Oh, you know it," Ella said with a wink.

They continued shopping together, exchanging decoration ideas and laughing over ridiculous items like a singing skeleton band and a creepy clown that made both of them shudder. Time flew by, and before they knew it, their baskets were full, and they were heading to the checkout line.

As they stood in line, Tom felt a sense of ease that was rare for him. He wasn't one to connect quickly with strangers, but with Ella, it was different. Their shared love for Halloween had sparked something more—a connection that felt special, like something out of a spooky, romantic movie.

As they parted ways outside the store, Tom couldn't help but glance back at her one last time. Ella waved, a soft smile playing on her lips as she disappeared into the crowd.

Tom turned toward his car, his heart lighter than it had been in a long time. Halloween was shaping up to be even better than he'd anticipated.

Chapter 2: A Hauntingly Good Start

Tom couldn't stop thinking about Ella. After their chance encounter at the Halloween store, he found himself replaying their conversation, her laugh, and the way her eyes sparkled when she talked about her love for Halloween. There was something about her—something magnetic. He had always thought meeting someone would be more complicated, but with Ella, it felt effortless.

A couple of days later, they had arranged to meet at a local coffee shop. It was a quaint little place, tucked away on a side street, with pumpkins and ghost-shaped string lights hanging in the windows. Tom arrived early, his stomach doing flips as he sat by the window, sipping a steaming cup of coffee and waiting for her.

Just as he was beginning to wonder if he was too early, the door jingled, and Ella walked in. She was bundled up in a cozy sweater, her cheeks flushed from the cool air outside, and she smiled warmly when she saw him. His heart skipped a beat.

"Hey, sorry I'm late," she said, taking a seat across from him. "I had a last-minute pumpkin crisis."

Tom raised an eyebrow, amused. "Pumpkin crisis?"

Ella laughed and rolled her eyes. "Yeah, I carved one last night, and this morning I found out my cat decided it was his new scratching post. So, I spent my morning cleaning up pumpkin guts all over my kitchen."

Tom chuckled. "Sounds like your cat's getting into the Halloween spirit, too."

"Oh, definitely. Every year, he thinks the decorations are his personal playground. It's a battle I'll never win," she said with a mock sigh, then added, "So, how's your decorating going? Did you get everything you needed?"

"Mostly," Tom replied, leaning back in his chair. "I still need to figure out how I'm going to set up the fog machine, though. It keeps malfunctioning. The last thing I want is for it to choke everyone with fake smoke."

Ella grinned. "I can give you a hand with that if you want. I've been known to be a bit of a fog machine expert. It's all about the placement and airflow."

"I'll take you up on that offer. You're officially hired as my Halloween consultant," Tom said, his smile widening.

As they sipped their drinks, the conversation flowed easily. They reminisced about their favorite Halloween memories, finding that they had much more in common than just their love for the holiday. Ella shared stories from her childhood, about how her mom would go all out with decorations, transforming their front yard into a graveyard complete with tombstones, cobwebs, and skeletons that danced. Every year, Ella would invite her friends over for a night of spooky fun, and they'd all help her mom make the house as creepy as possible.

"It's always been a big deal for us," Ella said, her voice filled with nostalgia. "We'd spend weeks planning everything, from the decorations to the costumes. I guess that's why Halloween has always been my favorite. It's more than just the costumes or candy. It's the whole atmosphere, you know? The excitement in the air, the way the world feels a little different, a little more magical."

Tom nodded, feeling a sense of connection as she spoke. "I get that. For me, it was always about the thrill of being someone else for a night. My friends and I would dress up as superheroes, monsters, or whatever we could come up with, and it felt like we were living in a different world. I guess Halloween always felt like an escape—like anything was possible for one night."

Ella smiled, her eyes softening. "Exactly. It's like the world lets its guard down, and you get to experience a little bit of magic."

As the conversation continued, they found themselves diving deeper into more personal territory. Ella spoke about her life in the city, how she'd moved there for work but stayed for the community and the vibrant, creative energy. She told Tom about her job as a graphic designer, and how Halloween always inspired her most artistic ideas.

"I feel like Halloween gives me the freedom to be as weird and creative as I want," she said with a laugh. "I've designed everything from haunted house flyers to spooky event posters. It's my busiest time of the year."

Tom was impressed. "That sounds amazing. I can barely draw a stick figure, so graphic design is like a superpower to me."

Ella shrugged, smiling modestly. "It's fun, and it keeps me busy. But enough about me—what about you? What do you do when you're not planning haunted houses?"

Tom hesitated for a moment, suddenly feeling a bit self-conscious. "I work in tech," he said. "Software development. It's not as creative as what you do, but it keeps the bills paid."

Ella leaned forward, her interest piqued. "That's still pretty cool. Do you ever get to design anything for Halloween events or anything fun like that?"

Tom chuckled. "Not really. I mostly work on boring business applications. But I guess you could say coding is its own kind of creativity."

"It absolutely is," Ella agreed. "There's a lot of creativity in problem-solving. Plus, you can always use those skills to build something spooky—like a haunted house app or a motion sensor for your decorations."

Tom raised his eyebrows, surprised by her insight. "You're giving me some ideas now."

Their conversation carried on for over an hour, drifting between lighthearted banter and deeper topics about life, work, and their passions. The connection between them was undeniable, and Tom could feel something special forming between them. It was rare for him to feel so comfortable with someone he'd just met, but with Ella, it was as if they'd known each other for much longer.

At one point, the waitress came by to refill their coffee cups, raising her eyebrows with a knowing smile when she noticed how engrossed they were in each other's company.

Eventually, Ella glanced at her watch and sighed. "I hate to cut this short, but I have to get back to work. Deadlines are looming."

Tom nodded, feeling a twinge of disappointment. He didn't want the moment to end. "Yeah, I should probably get back to reality, too. But this was fun. We should do it again."

Ella smiled, her eyes bright. "I'd like that."

As they stood to leave, Tom felt a strange sense of excitement bubbling inside him. He'd had plenty of good conversations with people before, but this felt different. There was something about Ella that made him want to spend more time with her, to learn more about her, and to see where this connection could lead.

Outside the coffee shop, they exchanged a quick hug—warm but not too intimate, just enough to suggest that they were both on the same page. As they pulled apart, Ella looked up at him, her eyes gleaming with something playful.

"So, when are we tackling that fog machine of yours?" she asked, her tone teasing.

Tom grinned. "How about tomorrow? You bring your expertise, and I'll provide the coffee."

"It's a deal," Ella said, and with that, she waved goodbye and walked off down the street.

Tom watched her go, a smile playing on his lips. He didn't know exactly what was going to happen between them, but for the first time in a long time, he felt hopeful—like maybe, just maybe, Halloween had brought a little magic into his life after all.

Chapter 3: The Halloween Decoration Hunt

The sun hung low in the sky as Tom made his way toward Ella's apartment. It was one of those perfect autumn days, where the streets were lined with fallen leaves, crunching underfoot, and every house seemed to be sporting some kind of Halloween decoration. Tom couldn't help but smile as he spotted a house with glowing pumpkins lined along its porch and a giant inflatable ghost waving in the breeze.

Ella had texted him earlier in the day, reminding him of their Halloween decoration shopping date. He was excited, not just because he loved Halloween, but because spending more time with Ella had quickly become something he looked forward to.

He knocked on her apartment door, and within seconds, Ella opened it, beaming with excitement. She was dressed casually in a soft black sweater and jeans, but Tom couldn't help but notice the playful Halloween-themed earrings dangling from her ears—tiny pumpkins that swayed as she moved.

"You ready for some serious Halloween shopping?" she asked with a grin.

"Absolutely," Tom said, returning her smile. "I hope you're prepared because I'm on a mission to find the perfect decorations."

Ella laughed and grabbed her bag. "Good! Let's hit the stores before all the best stuff gets snatched up."

They decided to start with a local craft store known for its elaborate holiday displays. As they walked inside, the smell of cinnamon and cloves greeted them once again, and Ella's eyes immediately lit up when she spotted a row of animated Halloween figures.

"Okay, we need to get one of these for sure," Ella said, pointing to a spooky animatronic witch that cackled and stirred a bubbling cauldron.

Tom raised an eyebrow. "Isn't that a bit over the top?"

Ella shook her head, her face serious, though her eyes were twinkling with mischief. "There is no 'over the top' when it comes to Halloween."

Tom laughed, realizing that was quickly becoming his favorite thing about Ella—her absolute love for the holiday and her ability to make everything fun. Together, they wandered through the aisles, pulling items off the shelves and tossing them into their cart.

"What do you think about this?" Tom asked, holding up a giant plastic spider with glowing red eyes.

Ella tilted her head, pretending to consider it seriously. "Hmm... it's creepy, but I feel like it needs a web to really sell it."

Tom grinned. "Good call. We'll get the webbing too. What about this?" He picked up a string of lights shaped like tiny bats.

Ella's face lit up again. "Perfect! Those would look amazing around your door."

They continued through the store, gathering items that fit both their styles—Tom leaning more toward eerie and classic, while Ella favored quirky and fun. By the time they reached the checkout, their cart was full of everything from tombstones and skulls to ghostly figures and decorative pumpkins.

"Do you always go this big for Halloween?" Tom asked as they loaded their purchases into his car.

"Every year," Ella said, laughing. "It's my one time to really go all out. It's like Christmas, but spookier."

"I like that," Tom said, closing the trunk and giving her a sidelong glance. "I've never been this serious about Halloween decorations before, but you've definitely inspired me."

"Well, I take that as a compliment," Ella said, playfully nudging him. "Besides, you can never have too many decorations. Trust me, when we're done, your apartment's going to look amazing."

Their next stop was a larger store that specialized in seasonal décor. This one was packed with customers, all just as eager to get their hands on the best Halloween items. As they walked through the entrance, Tom was immediately drawn to a large inflatable pumpkin archway, which stood tall in front of a display of life-sized skeletons.

"Now this is what I'm talking about," Tom said, pointing to the archway.

Ella looked it over, clearly impressed. "Okay, that's awesome. Imagine that at the entrance to your apartment. It'd be like welcoming people into a haunted house."

Tom laughed. "Exactly what I was thinking. Do you think we can fit this in the car?"

Ella tilted her head, pretending to measure it with her eyes. "It'll be a squeeze, but I think we can make it work."

They wandered through the store, getting lost in the variety of decorations. They picked out a few more items, including a fog machine that Ella promised she'd help set up, a string of eerie lanterns, and even a few creepy soundtracks that Tom thought would add to the atmosphere. Every time they found something particularly spooky, they'd excitedly show it to the other, exchanging ideas about how they could set it up.

As they stood in line at the checkout, Ella tapped Tom on the shoulder. "So, what's your grand plan? Are you turning your apartment into a haunted house or just giving it a spooky vibe?"

"I was thinking haunted house," Tom said, grinning. "But now that we've got all this stuff, I might end up turning it into a full-blown Halloween attraction."

Ella laughed. "I like the ambition. We'll definitely need to set aside a whole day for this."

After paying for their purchases and struggling to fit everything into the car, they decided to grab a quick bite to eat before heading back to Tom's apartment. Over burgers and fries, they continued brainstorming decoration ideas, and it wasn't long before their conversation shifted into memories from past Halloweens.

"You know," Ella began, "one of my favorite Halloween memories is when I was about ten years old. My mom and I spent the entire day turning our house into a haunted mansion. We had fake cobwebs everywhere, creepy music playing, and I even dressed up as a ghost to scare the kids who came trick-or-treating."

Tom smiled, imagining the scene. "Did it work?"

"Oh, totally," Ella said, her eyes sparkling with excitement. "There was this one group of older kids who thought they were too cool to be scared. So, I hid behind the door and jumped out just as they were walking up to the porch. They screamed so loud, they ran halfway down the street."

Tom chuckled. "That's impressive. I never managed to scare anyone that badly."

Ella shrugged playfully. "I've had a lot of practice."

After finishing their meal, they headed back to Tom's apartment, ready to begin the transformation. As they carried bags of decorations inside, Tom looked around the living room, feeling both excited and slightly overwhelmed.

"You think we went overboard?" he asked, glancing at the massive pile of decorations.

Ella shook her head, her expression serious. "There's no such thing as overboard when it comes to Halloween. Trust me, once we get started, you'll see."

As they began unpacking the decorations, Ella turned to him with a playful smile. "Okay, let's get spooky."

Tom laughed. "Let's do it."

Chapter 4: The Pumpkin Patch Date

Today was their first official date at the local pumpkin patch, and Tom felt a mix of excitement and nerves as he waited for Ella by the entrance.

He spotted her before she saw him, standing near a row of freshly picked pumpkins. She wore a deep orange scarf, a color that complemented the surrounding landscape of fiery autumn leaves and bright orange pumpkins. She was smiling as she waved at him, and Tom felt his heart skip a beat.

"You made it!" she called out as she approached, her cheeks flushed from the cool air.

"I wouldn't miss it," Tom said with a grin, his nerves easing as soon as they started talking. There was something about Ella that put him at ease, like everything was natural and easy between them.

She glanced around at the rows of pumpkins, the farmstand offering hot cider, and the nearby hayrides filled with laughing families. "Isn't this place perfect? I've been coming here every year since I moved to the city. It's kind of a tradition now."

"I can see why," Tom said, taking in the atmosphere. It was the perfect blend of nostalgia and fun, and he could already feel the excitement building for their afternoon adventure. "So, what's the plan? Do we pick the biggest pumpkin, or are we going for something unique?"

Ella smiled mischievously. "Oh, I'm all about finding the perfect pumpkin—one with a little personality. I never go for the biggest. It's more about the character."

Tom laughed. "Character, huh? Well, I'm in. Let's find some pumpkins with personality."

They walked side by side through the pumpkin patch, stopping every now and then to examine a particularly interesting one. Some were tall and thin, while others were squat and wide, each with its own distinct charm. The wind rustled through the trees, carrying with it the sound of children's laughter and the faint hum of a nearby tractor pulling a hayride.

"So, do you have a go-to design for your jack-o'-lanterns?" Ella asked, squatting down to inspect a perfectly round pumpkin with a crooked stem.

"Usually just the classic face—triangle eyes, toothy grin," Tom replied, watching as she tested the weight of the pumpkin in her hands. "I'm not much of an artist, but I make up for it in enthusiasm."

Ella grinned. "Enthusiasm is half the battle. I like to get creative with mine. Last year, I carved one that looked like a cat, complete with pointy ears."

Tom raised an eyebrow, impressed. "Now that's impressive. You'll have to give me some tips. I might be able to handle a toothy grin, but a cat might be out of my league."

She laughed and handed him the pumpkin. "Here, test this one. It has good weight, and the shape is perfect for a spooky design."

Tom took the pumpkin from her, marveling at how light it felt despite its size. "You've got an eye for this," he said. "I can see why you're the Halloween consultant."

Ella winked. "It's a gift."

They spent the next hour picking out their pumpkins, comparing shapes and imagining the faces they'd carve. At one point, Ella found a tiny pumpkin, no bigger than her hand, and held it up to Tom with a playful grin.

"This one has personality," she declared. "Look at the little guy."

Tom chuckled, taking the tiny pumpkin from her and pretending to examine it seriously. "Definitely a lot of character here. This one might be the star of the night."

After choosing their pumpkins, they wandered over to the farmstand for a cup of warm apple cider. Tom held his cup between his hands, savoring the warmth as they found a spot near the hay bales to sit and enjoy the view.

Ella took a sip of her cider, closing her eyes for a moment as if savoring the taste. "This is what I love about fall," she said softly. "Everything just feels... right. You know?"

Tom nodded, looking out over the pumpkin patch and the families enjoying the day. "Yeah, I get that. There's something about this time of year that feels like a reset, like everything slows down a bit."

They sat in comfortable silence for a while, watching the sun begin to dip lower in the sky, casting long shadows over the field. Tom felt a sense of peace he hadn't experienced in a long time. It wasn't just the perfect fall day or the atmosphere of the pumpkin patch—it was being here with Ella, sharing something simple yet meaningful.

As the sky turned a soft shade of pink, Ella glanced at Tom with a smile. "Want to carve these pumpkins back at your place? I think we've got some masterpieces waiting to be made."

Tom's heart did a little flip at the thought of spending more time with her. "Absolutely. My apartment's ready for a pumpkin carving session."

They gathered their pumpkins and made their way back to Tom's car, laughing as they struggled to fit all of their pumpkin loot into the backseat. The drive back to his apartment was filled with more easy conversation, and by the time they arrived, the sun had set, casting an orange glow over the skyline.

Inside his apartment, the air was cool and inviting. Tom had already set up a table with newspapers spread out and all the necessary carving tools at the ready. Ella looked around, impressed. "Wow, you really came prepared," she said, her eyes sparkling.

"I figured you'd appreciate it," Tom said, smiling. "I've got everything we need, including some spooky background music."

Ella laughed as he hit play on a playlist full of eerie Halloween sounds, complete with howling winds, ghostly whispers, and the occasional creaking door. "This is perfect," she said, grabbing a carving tool and setting her pumpkin on the table. "Let's get started."

For the next hour, they carved their pumpkins, laughing as they compared designs and teased each other about their carving skills. Tom's jack-o'-lantern was, as he predicted, a classic toothy grin, while Ella's featured an intricate spiderweb pattern that she carved with surprising precision.

"I have to say, I'm impressed," Tom said, admiring her work. "You weren't kidding about being creative."

Ella shrugged, her eyes twinkling with pride. "It's all in the details. Yours has that classic charm, though. It's timeless."

They placed the finished jack-o'-lanterns on the windowsill, lighting them up with small LED candles. As the soft glow illuminated their carved designs, Tom felt a sense of accomplishment. But more than that, he felt something deeper—a connection with Ella that went beyond just their shared love of Halloween.

Chapter 5: Spooky Movie Marathon

The wind howled outside Tom's apartment, rattling the windows and sending a chill through the air. Inside, however, it was warm and cozy, with the faint scent of popcorn drifting through the living room. Tom glanced around, making sure everything was ready for the evening ahead. The lights were dimmed, casting shadows that danced across the Halloween decorations they'd hung earlier that week—fake cobwebs, flickering candles, and Ella's favorite addition: a string of glowing bat-shaped lights along the wall.

It was their first official Halloween movie marathon together, and Tom was determined to make it perfect.

He had spent the afternoon picking out an assortment of classic horror films, ranging from the iconic slasher flicks of the '80s to the more atmospheric and chilling ghost stories of the '60s. He wasn't sure what kind of movies Ella preferred, so he'd gone for variety—something scary, something campy, and something downright terrifying.

The doorbell rang, and Tom's heart did a little flip. He wiped his hands on his jeans, trying to shake off the excitement that seemed to bubble up every time he saw Ella. When he opened the door, she was standing there, bundled up in a scarf and holding a bag of snacks.

"Hey!" Ella greeted him with a bright smile. "Hope you're ready for some serious scares. I brought reinforcements," she said, lifting the bag of candy and homemade Halloween cookies she'd baked earlier that day. "You can't watch horror movies without a sugar rush, right?"

Tom grinned, stepping aside to let her in. "Absolutely. You're speaking my language."

Ella took off her scarf and coat, revealing a cute, oversized sweater with little black cats embroidered on it. "Nice decorations," she said, glancing around the room. "You've really got the spooky vibe going on."

"Thanks. I had to step up my game after all the tips you gave me," Tom said, leading her into the living room where he'd set up blankets and pillows on the couch for maximum comfort. "I figured we could start with something classic, maybe work our way up to the really scary stuff."

Ella laughed as she set the snacks down on the coffee table. "I love it. What's first on the list?"

Tom held up a DVD case of *Psycho*. "How about some Hitchcock to kick things off?"

Ella's eyes lit up. "Perfect choice. Suspenseful, creepy, but not too much gore. Great way to ease into the night."

Tom popped the DVD into the player and grabbed the remote, settling onto the couch beside Ella. The room grew quiet as the iconic music from the opening credits of *Psycho* filled the space, setting the mood for the evening. They sat in comfortable silence for the first few minutes of the film, the tension on-screen mirrored by the slow build of excitement between them.

About halfway through the movie, when the infamous shower scene began to unfold, Tom noticed Ella shifting a little closer to him, her eyes wide as she gripped the edge of the blanket they were sharing.

"You've seen this one before, right?" Tom asked, glancing at her with a teasing smile.

"Of course," she whispered, her gaze never leaving the screen. "But it never gets any less intense."

Just as the knife came down in the film, accompanied by those sharp, screeching violins, Ella flinched, and Tom couldn't help but laugh. She shot him a playful glare.

"What? It's a classic scare," Tom said, holding up his hands in mock innocence.

Ella rolled her eyes but laughed along with him. "Okay, fine. But if you get jumpy later, I'm totally teasing you."

"Deal," Tom agreed, enjoying the ease with which they teased each other. There was something about spending time with Ella that made everything feel lighter, even when they were watching terrifying movies.

As *Psycho* came to an end, Ella reached for one of the cookies she had brought. "Alright, time for something a little more fun. What's next on the list?"

Tom grinned, holding up a copy of *Hocus Pocus*. "How about a Halloween classic that's less scary and more... nostalgic?"

Ella's face lit up with excitement. "Yes! I love *Hocus Pocus*! I watch it every year. It's not Halloween without it."

Tom put the movie on, and soon they were laughing along with the misadventures of the Sanderson sisters, their spooky antics providing a lighthearted contrast to the tension of the previous film. As the movie played, they traded stories about their favorite Halloween traditions from childhood—Tom talked about trick-or-treating in his old neighborhood, while Ella reminisced about watching scary movies with her friends during sleepovers, armed with bowls of popcorn and flashlights to ward off the dark.

"I used to be terrified after watching horror movies as a kid," Ella admitted, giggling. "I couldn't sleep for days after watching *The Exorcist*. I kept thinking my bed was going to levitate."

Tom chuckled. "Yeah, that one's intense. I think the first movie that really got to me was *The Shining*. Something about those creepy twins..."

Ella shuddered dramatically. "Ugh, the twins! I couldn't walk down long hallways for a week after that."

They continued swapping movie stories as the credits rolled on *Hocus Pocus*, the conversation flowing effortlessly between them. Tom glanced at the clock, realizing how late it was getting, but neither of them seemed ready to call it a night.

"Alright," Ella said, stretching and reaching for another cookie. "We've done suspense, we've done nostalgia… I think it's time for something that'll actually scare us. What's your scariest pick?"

Tom raised an eyebrow. "You sure you're ready for it?"

Ella grinned, clearly up for the challenge. "I can handle it."

With a mischievous smile, Tom pulled out the final movie of the night—*The Conjuring*. "This one gets me every time," he admitted, holding up the DVD case. "It's got the right amount of paranormal creepiness without being over the top."

Ella's eyes widened in approval. "Oh, yes. Now we're talking."

Tom dimmed the lights even further and started the movie. From the very first scene, the tension in the room began to build. The eerie, unsettling atmosphere of the film set both of them on edge. Tom could feel Ella shift closer to him as the story unfolded, the air between them charged with anticipation.

At one point, during one of the film's quieter, more suspenseful moments, a loud bang from the kitchen caused both of them to jump. Ella grabbed Tom's arm, her eyes wide with alarm. "What was that?" she whispered.

Tom laughed, his heart still racing. "Probably just the wind. Or, you know, the ghost that lives here."

Ella smirked, though her grip on his arm didn't loosen. "Very funny."

As the movie reached its terrifying climax, with all the supernatural activity coming to a head, Tom could feel the tension between them shift from fear to something else—something unspoken, but undeniable. When the credits finally rolled, they both let out a breath they hadn't realized they'd been holding.

"Well," Ella said, leaning back against the couch. "That was terrifying. And amazing."

"Agreed," Tom said, feeling a mixture of adrenaline and contentment. "I'm glad we survived it."

Ella laughed softly. "Barely."

They sat in the comfortable quiet for a moment, the tension of the movie fading into a calm, peaceful atmosphere. Tom glanced over at her, realizing that the night had been perfect—not just because of the movies, but because of her.

"I had a really great time tonight," Ella said softly, catching his gaze.

"Me too," Tom replied, his voice just as quiet.

For a moment, they just looked at each other, the flickering light from the jack-o'-lanterns casting soft shadows on their faces. There was a feeling between them now, something electric, but neither of them rushed it. It felt like the beginning of something... something just as exciting and magical as the Halloween season itself.

Chapter 6: Haunted Hayride

The night was perfect for a haunted hayride. The moon hung low in the sky, casting a pale, silvery light over the sprawling farmland, and a crisp chill filled the air. Tom pulled his jacket tighter as he and Ella made their way toward the starting point for the hayride, their breath visible in the cool autumn air.

Ella was practically bouncing with excitement. "I've been looking forward to this all week! Haunted hayrides are the best."

Tom grinned, watching her enthusiasm bubble over. "I can't believe I've never done one before. I've been to haunted houses, but never a hayride."

"You're in for a treat," Ella said, her eyes twinkling mischievously. "It's like a haunted house, but on wheels. Spooky stuff comes at you from every angle, and there's nowhere to hide. It's the best kind of scare."

They reached the starting point, where several other groups of people were already lined up, waiting to board the large, open wagon filled with hay bales. The air was thick with anticipation and the distant sound of chainsaws and eerie music from the hayride's course, just barely audible over the murmur of the crowd.

Tom noticed Ella scanning the line of people. "Looking for someone?"

She smiled, shaking her head. "No, just scoping out the competition. Some people get really freaked out on these rides. It's kind of fun to watch."

Tom chuckled. "Let me guess, you're one of those people who stays totally calm while everyone else screams?"

"Maybe," she said, grinning playfully. "Or maybe I'm just really good at hiding my fear."

Soon, the wagon pulled up to the boarding area, and the excited chatter around them grew louder. The wagon itself was decorated with tattered cloth and fake cobwebs, adding to the spooky atmosphere. The hay bales looked like they'd been used for several rides, with tufts of straw sticking out in all directions, creating the perfect setting for what was to come.

Tom and Ella climbed aboard, finding a spot near the middle of the wagon. They settled onto the hay, their knees brushing as they got comfortable. Tom noticed Ella glance around at the other riders, some of whom were already nervously clutching the edges of their seats.

As the tractor roared to life and the wagon began to lurch forward, the excitement among the passengers grew. The ride started out calm enough, with the tractor pulling them through a darkened path lined with cornfields and twisted, leafless trees. The only sound was the creaking of the wagon wheels and the occasional whisper of the wind through the cornstalks.

"Not so scary yet," Tom said, leaning closer to Ella.

"Just wait," she whispered back. "The quiet is always the worst part."

And she was right. The silence was unnerving, making every little sound—every snap of a twig or rustle of the corn—seem more menacing. Tom glanced around, feeling the tension build. He wasn't easily scared, but there was something about the isolation of the hayride, the way they were out in the middle of nowhere, with nothing but darkness and shadows surrounding them.

Suddenly, without warning, a figure dressed as a ghoulish zombie leapt out of the cornfields, slamming its hands against the side of the wagon. A few people screamed, and Tom felt Ella jump slightly beside him, though she quickly recovered, grinning as the zombie dragged a rusted chainsaw across the ground, creating a terrible screeching noise.

"I told you, it's all about the surprises," Ella said, laughing softly.

Tom smiled, though he could feel his heart racing a little. He wasn't about to admit it, but the sudden jump-scares were more effective than he'd expected. As the wagon continued along the path, more figures began to emerge from the corn—ghostly specters, rotting zombies, and grotesque creatures that seemed to materialize out of nowhere, all of them adding to the growing sense of unease.

At one point, the tractor came to a sudden stop near an old, run-down barn. The passengers all fell silent, their eyes glued to the dark structure looming ahead of them. Tom could feel the tension in the air as they waited for the next scare.

"What do you think's inside?" Ella whispered, her voice barely audible over the nervous murmurs of the crowd.

Tom shook his head. "I'm guessing something terrifying."

As if on cue, the barn doors creaked open, revealing a dimly lit interior filled with fog. Slowly, the wagon began to move again, inching its way closer to the entrance. Tom could feel his heart thudding in his chest, and he glanced over at Ella, who was watching the barn with wide eyes, her excitement palpable.

Just as they crossed the threshold, a figure burst out of the fog—a monstrous clown with a menacing grin, wielding a giant mallet. The clown slammed the mallet down on a nearby crate, sending a loud bang echoing through the barn. Several people screamed, and Tom instinctively reached for Ella's hand, gripping it tightly as they were plunged into darkness.

He felt Ella squeeze his hand back, her grip reassuring even as the chaos unfolded around them. The wagon passed through the barn, where more figures appeared from the shadows—creepy dolls, snarling werewolves, and faceless ghouls that seemed to melt in and out of the fog.

By the time they emerged on the other side, Tom was both exhilarated and relieved. He released Ella's hand, realizing he'd been holding onto it the entire time.

"That... was intense," he said, trying to catch his breath.

Ella laughed, brushing some hay off her lap. "Told you it was fun. You handled it like a pro, though."

Tom smiled, feeling a little sheepish. "Yeah, well... you weren't exactly screaming either."

"I told you, I've got nerves of steel," she said, though the mischievous glint in her eyes suggested otherwise.

As the ride continued, the scares became more frequent and more elaborate. At one point, the wagon passed by a makeshift graveyard, where tombstones rattled and skeletal hands reached up from the ground. A fog machine hissed, filling the air with an eerie mist, and ghostly figures floated between the trees, their mournful wails echoing in the distance.

Ella leaned closer to Tom, her voice low. "This is my favorite part. I love the graveyard scenes. They always have the best atmosphere."

Tom nodded, agreeing. There was something about the fog, the dim lighting, and the way the shadows played off the tombstones that made the whole scene feel otherworldly, like they were truly being transported into a world of the dead.

As the ride neared its end, the final scare came in the form of a towering figure—an enormous, masked creature wielding a bloody axe. It stood in the middle of the path, blocking their way, forcing the tractor to slow to a crawl. The creature's head turned slowly, its glowing eyes locking onto the passengers in the wagon. Then, with a deafening roar, it charged forward, slamming the axe into the ground just inches from the wheels.

The entire wagon screamed as the creature roared again, but Tom found himself laughing, the adrenaline and thrill of the moment washing over him. He glanced over at Ella, who was laughing as well, her eyes bright with excitement.

"That was incredible!" she said as the ride finally came to a stop, and the tractor pulled them back toward the entrance.

Tom couldn't agree more. As they climbed off the wagon and made their way toward the parking lot, he felt an overwhelming sense of joy.

The night had been thrilling, filled with scares and laughter, but the best part had been sharing it all with Ella.

As they walked back to the car, Ella slipped her hand into his, squeezing it lightly. "Thanks for coming with me tonight," she said softly.

Tom smiled, squeezing her hand back. "Thanks for inviting me. I had a blast."

Chapter 7: The Halloween Costume Decision

Tom stood in front of his closet, staring blankly at the few costumes he had accumulated over the years. There wasn't much to choose from—a pirate hat, a tattered vampire cape from a party long ago, and a rubber zombie mask that had seen better days. It was clear he needed something new this year, especially now that he and Ella had agreed to dress up for the upcoming Halloween party at their friend Matt's house.

But the real challenge was finding a matching costume.

Ever since their conversation about the party a few days ago, Tom had been trying to come up with ideas. Ella had playfully suggested they go as a couple's costume—something fun, something that matched their personalities, but nothing too cheesy. The problem was, Tom was completely stuck on what that could be.

Just as he was about to text Ella for advice, his phone buzzed on the nightstand. He picked it up and smiled when he saw her name on the screen.

Ella: "I'm bringing over some costume ideas. Be there in 10! ◇"

Tom laughed to himself, already feeling a sense of relief. Ella had a knack for creativity, and he was more than willing to let her lead the charge on this one. He quickly tidied up his living room and set out a few snacks on the coffee table, knowing their brainstorming session might turn into a longer conversation.

Within minutes, there was a knock at the door. Tom opened it to find Ella standing there, grinning and holding a shopping bag that looked like it was bursting at the seams. She stepped inside, her eyes gleaming with excitement.

"I hope you're ready to make some decisions," Ella said, placing the bag on the couch and pulling out a variety of costume pieces. "Because I've got options."

Tom laughed, already feeling more at ease. "I'm ready. Show me what you've got."

Ella wasted no time diving into her ideas. She pulled out the first option—a pair of matching wizard and witch costumes. The robes were dark and flowing, with stars and moons embroidered along the edges, and Ella had even brought a set of wands to complete the look.

"I was thinking we could go as a wizard and witch," she explained, twirling one of the wands in her hand. "It's classic, and you know, magic is always a good Halloween theme."

Tom nodded thoughtfully. "I like it. Definitely gives off that spooky vibe."

Ella smiled but quickly moved on to the next option. "Okay, but if that's too traditional for you, I also picked up these."

She pulled out two costumes that immediately made Tom grin—one was a classic vampire outfit, complete with a cape and fake fangs, and the other was a vampire slayer, with leather belts, wooden stakes, and a cross necklace.

"We could do a vampire and vampire hunter," Ella said, clearly excited about this idea. "It's kind of like a battle of good versus evil, but in a fun, Halloween-y way."

Tom raised an eyebrow, intrigued. "That's actually pretty awesome. I'd get to wear a cape, which is always a plus."

Ella laughed, tossing the cape over his shoulders playfully. "See? You're already getting into it."

As Tom admired the cape in the mirror, he couldn't help but notice how much fun Ella was having. Her energy was infectious, and he found himself getting excited about the costumes, too. He turned back to her, a grin on his face.

"What else have you got?" he asked.

Ella's eyes sparkled mischievously as she reached into the bag for the final option. "Okay, this one is more of a wild card, but I thought it could be fun."

She pulled out two matching skeleton onesies, complete with glow-in-the-dark bones and hooded masks that resembled grinning skulls. Tom burst out laughing.

"Skeletons?" he asked, holding up one of the suits.

Ella nodded, her expression playful. "Hear me out. It's simple, it's spooky, and we'd totally match. Plus, we'd glow in the dark."

Tom laughed again, imagining the two of them showing up at the party in matching skeleton costumes. It was both ridiculous and kind of perfect. He liked that it didn't take itself too seriously, which fit with the easygoing vibe they'd developed as a couple.

"I actually love this," Tom said, still chuckling. "It's fun. We wouldn't be trying too hard, and it's definitely Halloween-worthy."

Ella beamed. "Right? I thought it'd be a good option. Plus, we could dance around like skeletons all night."

Tom shook his head, still smiling. "You're ridiculous."

Ella laughed, plopping down on the couch beside him. "So, what do you think? Any favorites? Wizard and witch, vampire and hunter, or glowing skeletons?"

Tom leaned back, considering the options. The truth was, he liked all of them. Each one had its own charm, and he loved how excited Ella had been about each idea. But there was something about the skeleton costumes that felt right—it was playful, unexpected, and they'd definitely stand out at the party.

"I think we should go with the skeletons," Tom said after a moment. "It's fun, and it'll make for some great pictures."

Ella's eyes lit up. "I'm so glad you said that! I was secretly hoping you'd pick the skeletons. I mean, look at these." She held up the glow-in-the-dark masks, waving them in front of him. "We'll be the life of the party—pun intended."

Tom groaned at her joke but couldn't help smiling. "Alright, let's do it. Skeletons it is."

They spent the next hour trying on the costumes, laughing as they posed in front of the mirror with their glowing bones. Ella gave Tom tips on how to make their costumes even better, suggesting they add a few spooky accessories—like fake cobwebs draped over their shoulders or some eerie face paint to make them look even more skeletal.

Chapter 8: The Halloween Party

The night of the Halloween party arrived, and Tom couldn't help but feel a rush of excitement as he stood in front of the mirror, adjusting his skeleton mask for the final time. The glow-in-the-dark bones on his onesie reflected faintly in the dim lighting of his apartment, and despite how ridiculous the costume might seem, he loved it. There was something freeing about dressing up, letting go of the everyday expectations and leaning into the playful, spooky side of the holiday.

Ella would be arriving any minute, and the thought of seeing her in her matching skeleton costume made him smile. Over the past week, they had shared excited texts and last-minute costume tweaks, and now, the night was finally here.

As if on cue, there was a knock at the door. Tom walked over and opened it, revealing Ella standing in the hallway, her glowing skeleton costume fully on display. She grinned up at him from beneath her mask, her eyes sparkling with excitement.

"Ready to get spooky?" she asked, her voice playful.

Tom laughed. "You look amazing. These costumes are perfect."

Ella twirled around, showing off her glowing bones. "I know, right? We're definitely going to be the highlight of the party."

Tom grabbed his keys and a small bag filled with snacks they'd agreed to bring to the party. "Let's go steal the show."

The party was at their friend Matt's house, which had become legendary for his elaborate Halloween bashes. Every year, Matt transformed his home into a Halloween wonderland, complete with cobweb-covered archways, animatronic monsters, and enough creepy lighting to make it feel like you were stepping into a haunted house.

As they approached Matt's place, Tom could already hear the low thrum of music and the excited chatter of partygoers. The house itself was decked out in a combination of eerie orange lighting and fog machines that spilled mist over the front lawn. A giant skeleton stood in the yard, towering over the guests as they made their way inside.

Ella linked her arm with Tom's as they approached the door, her excitement bubbling over. "I love what Matt's done with the place. It's even more over the top than last year."

Tom nodded, taking in the scene. "It's like stepping into a haunted theme park."

They pushed through the front door and were immediately greeted by a swirl of costumes, laughter, and the smell of freshly baked pumpkin pie. The living room was packed with people dressed as everything from classic movie monsters to quirky, homemade costumes. A DJ in the corner was playing a spooky playlist, and the entire room was bathed in dim, flickering light that made the decorations look even more eerie.

"Tom! Ella!" Matt's voice boomed from across the room. He was dressed as Dracula this year, his cape billowing as he made his way over to them. "I knew you two would come through with the costumes. Those skeleton onesies are awesome."

"Thanks, Matt," Tom said, laughing. "We went for the glowing effect."

Ella raised her arms, showing off the glow-in-the-dark bones. "You can't go wrong with skeletons."

Matt grinned. "You guys look great. Grab a drink, make yourselves at home. There's a costume contest later, so be sure to stick around."

Tom exchanged a glance with Ella, both of them grinning. "We'll definitely be there," Ella said, her competitive spirit shining through.

They moved deeper into the party, weaving through groups of costumed guests, their skeleton costumes earning plenty of compliments along the way. Tom felt at ease with Ella by his side, enjoying the energy of the party and the shared excitement of celebrating Halloween together.

After grabbing drinks from the kitchen, they found a spot near the fireplace, where the glow of the flames gave the room an extra eerie atmosphere. Ella looked around, taking in the decorations with wide-eyed admiration.

"Matt really outdid himself this year," she said, sipping her drink. "I mean, look at that ghost over there. It looks like it's floating in midair."

Tom followed her gaze and nodded in agreement. "It's impressive. He always goes all out for this party."

As the night went on, they mingled with other guests, laughing at the creative costumes and joining in on Halloween-themed party games. At one point, they found themselves in a spirited game of Halloween trivia, competing against a group dressed as zombies and witches. Ella's knowledge of all things spooky helped them score major points, and by the end of the game, they were crowned the winners, much to their delight.

"I knew all those horror movies would come in handy one day," Ella said with a grin, holding up their prize—a bottle of pumpkin-flavored liqueur.

"I'm glad you were on my team," Tom replied, laughing. "I wouldn't have stood a chance without you."

As they moved back into the main living room, the DJ announced that the costume contest would be starting soon. Ella's eyes lit up with excitement, and Tom couldn't help but feel a surge of competitive energy as well.

"We've got this," Ella said confidently, adjusting her glowing mask. "There's no way anyone else can compete with our skeleton moves."

Tom chuckled. "Let's do it."

The contest began with each couple or individual stepping into the center of the room to show off their costumes. Some people had gone all out with elaborate getups—there was a couple dressed as Frankenstein and his bride, another group of friends dressed as superheroes, and even a man wearing an impressive, homemade robot costume.

But when it was Tom and Ella's turn, they played it up, twirling around and making their glowing skeletons dance in the dim lighting. The room erupted in cheers and laughter, and by the end of their little performance, Tom could tell they'd made an impression.

"Wow," the DJ announced as they finished. "Those skeletons are glowing! Give it up for the best-dressed couple here tonight!"

The crowd cheered, and Tom felt a wave of pride as he glanced at Ella, her face beaming with joy. They hadn't won any official prize, but the reaction from the crowd was enough. The fun and lightheartedness of their performance perfectly captured the spirit of the night.

Afterward, as the party wound down and guests began to filter out, Tom and Ella found themselves back near the fireplace, basking in the glow of the evening's fun. Ella leaned back against the couch, her eyes still twinkling with excitement.

"This was perfect," she said softly, glancing at Tom. "I had so much fun."

Tom smiled, feeling the same way. "Me too. I think this might be the best Halloween party I've ever been to."

Ella tilted her head, a playful smile on her lips. "You know, we make a pretty good team."

"I was thinking the same thing," Tom replied, his voice softening.

They sat in comfortable silence for a moment, the warmth of the fireplace and the lingering buzz of the party wrapping around them like a blanket. Tom couldn't help but feel that this night had been a turning point, not just for the fun they'd had, but for the connection that had deepened between them.

Ella glanced at him, her eyes catching the flickering firelight. "We should make this a tradition. Every Halloween, new costumes, new adventures."

Tom grinned, nodding. "I'm all in."

In that moment, surrounded by the fading sounds of the party and the warmth of their shared experience, Tom knew that this Halloween had been more than just a fun night—it had been the start of something special, something that felt right.

Chapter 9: Trick-or-Treat for Adults

The day after the Halloween party, Tom woke up with a sense of contentment, his mind still buzzing from the fun they had the previous night. As he sipped his morning coffee, a notification popped up on his phone—a message from Ella.

Ella: "So... how do you feel about a trick-or-treat adventure for adults? 😈"

Tom raised an eyebrow and smiled. He quickly typed back.

Tom: "I'm intrigued. What's the plan?"

Ella responded almost immediately.

Ella: "Meet me at the corner of Elm and Oak at 7. I've got something fun in mind. Bring your sense of adventure. 😈"

Tom laughed, knowing that with Ella, whatever she had planned was bound to be a good time. The excitement of Halloween hadn't died down after the party—it had only just begun.

By the time the evening rolled around, Tom found himself standing at the corner of Elm and Oak, as instructed, dressed warmly in his jacket and scarf. He had no idea what to expect from this "trick-or-treat adventure for adults," but knowing Ella, it would be creative and full of surprises.

He didn't have to wait long. A few minutes later, Ella appeared, walking briskly down the street with a wide grin on her face. She was dressed in a cozy black coat, her hair tucked beneath a witch's hat—an amusing nod to the holiday that made Tom smile.

"Ready for some Halloween fun?" she asked as she approached, her eyes gleaming with excitement.

"Always," Tom said, curiosity piqued. "So, what exactly do you have planned?"

Ella gestured toward the street behind her. "I've set up a kind of trick-or-treat scavenger hunt for us. I thought it would be fun to relive some of that childhood magic, but with an adult twist."

Tom raised an eyebrow, intrigued. "A scavenger hunt?"

"Exactly," Ella replied, holding up a small envelope. "We'll visit some houses around the neighborhood—ones I've picked out ahead of time. At each stop, there's a Halloween-themed surprise waiting for us. And yes, there will be candy, but there are also other surprises that aren't quite so... sugary."

Tom grinned. "I love it. So what's the first stop?"

Ella handed him the envelope, a mischievous smile playing on her lips. "Open it and find out."

Tom carefully opened the envelope, pulling out a small card with a clue written on it:

"To find the first treat, head to the house that has the most fright. Its pumpkins glow orange, and its ghosts are white."

Tom read the clue out loud, and Ella laughed, nodding toward the direction of the house. "I think you'll recognize it once you see it. Come on, let's go!"

They started down the street together, the cool autumn air making their breath visible as they walked. The neighborhood was still buzzing with the remnants of Halloween—jack-o'-lanterns flickered on porches, and a few late-night trick-or-treaters roamed the streets in their costumes. The air felt charged with that special kind of energy that only came around this time of year.

After a few minutes, Tom spotted the house described in the clue. It was a large, old-fashioned Victorian home, decked out in elaborate Halloween decorations. Pumpkins lined the walkway, their glowing faces flickering with eerie light, and ghosts made from billowing white sheets hung from the porch.

"Found it," Tom said, pointing to the house.

Ella smiled, clearly impressed. "Good job. Now let's see what the surprise is."

They walked up to the house, and as they approached the front door, a bowl of candy greeted them on the porch. But next to the candy was a small, neatly wrapped package with their names on it.

Ella picked it up, her curiosity piqued. "Well, well, what do we have here?"

Tom grinned. "Open it."

Ella carefully unwrapped the package, revealing two small bottles of spiced pumpkin liqueur along with a note that read, *"For the adults who still love Halloween. Enjoy a little liquid treat!"*

Ella laughed, holding up the bottles. "Looks like our first treat isn't candy after all."

Tom chuckled, feeling the warmth of the liqueur already. "I'm not complaining. This is a pretty sweet start."

They toasted with the tiny bottles, savoring the rich, spicy flavor of the liqueur. The warmth spread through Tom's chest as he swallowed, and the feeling of nostalgia mixed with the grown-up twist on trick-or-treating made the experience even more enjoyable.

"Ready for the next stop?" Ella asked, her excitement still evident.

Tom nodded eagerly. "Let's do it."

Ella handed him the second envelope, and together they read the next clue, which directed them to a house with a yard full of "creepy crawlers and spiders that glow."

As they made their way to the next house, Tom found himself marveling at Ella's creativity. She had managed to take something as simple as trick-or-treating and turn it into a fun, engaging adventure for the two of them, complete with surprises that made him feel like a kid again—but with an added twist of grown-up fun.

They arrived at the next house, where, true to the clue, the yard was filled with oversized plastic spiders glowing under black lights. Ella approached the front porch, where another envelope awaited them along with a selection of Halloween-themed cocktails in mini mason jars.

"This is amazing," Tom said, admiring the spooky drinks.

Ella grinned, handing him one. "Cheers to Halloween magic, even for adults."

They toasted again and enjoyed the drinks as they continued on their scavenger hunt, moving from house to house. Each stop held a new surprise—some offering more candy, others presenting small, festive treats like mini pumpkin pies or bags of homemade caramel popcorn. One stop even had a setup for them to take Halloween photos in front of an elaborate haunted backdrop, which they happily posed for, laughing at how ridiculous they looked in their costumes.

By the time they reached the final house on the list, Tom's face ached from smiling so much. The last clue had led them to a house at the edge of the neighborhood, where a fog machine billowed mist across the lawn, and eerie green lights flickered from the windows. On the porch was a pumpkin carved with intricate details, and sitting beside it was one last envelope.

Tom opened it and read the note inside:

"For the final treat, look behind the gate. There's something sweet awaiting your fate."

Ella nudged him with her elbow, clearly excited to see what it was. Together, they walked around the side of the house, following the mist until they reached a small, wrought-iron gate. Beyond it was a small table set with two cups of hot apple cider, steam rising from the surface.

Tom smiled, feeling a surge of warmth. "Cider to end the night?"

Ella replied. "A perfect way to end our adult trick-or-treat adventure."

They sat down on a nearby bench, sipping their warm cider as the fog swirled around them, the night peaceful and quiet now that most of the trick-or-treaters had gone home. The moon hung high in the sky, casting a soft glow over the houses, and Tom felt a deep sense of contentment wash over him.

"This was amazing," he said after a few minutes of comfortable silence. "You're seriously the queen of Halloween."

Ella laughed, her eyes bright. "I just wanted to do something fun, something that made us feel like kids again. But I think I like this adult version even better."

With a heart full, Tom replied. "Same here. This was perfect."

As they finished their cider, they walked back through the neighborhood, hand in hand.

Chapter 10: Visiting a Real Haunted House

Tom pulled up to Ella's apartment, his heart beating with a mix of excitement and nerves. Tonight was different from their usual Halloween fun. This wasn't about decorations, parties, or costumes. Tonight, Ella had planned something with a bit more mystery—a visit to a real haunted house.

He wasn't the type to scare easily, but the idea of visiting a place with an actual history of hauntings had a way of creeping into his mind. He couldn't deny he was curious, though. When Ella had suggested it, he had immediately agreed. It was another adventure, and he was always up for that, especially with her.

Ella emerged from her apartment a few minutes later, looking more casual than usual. She wore a dark jacket, a simple scarf, and jeans, but the excitement in her eyes made it clear that tonight was going to be anything but ordinary.

"Are you ready for this?" she asked as she climbed into the passenger seat, her voice full of excitement.

Tom smiled, though he could feel his nerves surfacing. "I think so. I mean, how haunted is this place, really?"

Ella grinned mischievously, her eyes sparkling in the dim streetlights. "Pretty haunted. It's an old Victorian mansion about half an hour outside the city. People say it's been haunted for years—ever since the original owners passed away under mysterious circumstances."

"Mysterious circumstances?" Tom raised an eyebrow, intrigued despite himself.

"Yeah, it's kind of a tragic story," Ella said as they pulled away from her building and began driving toward the haunted mansion. "The house was owned by a wealthy couple in the late 1800s. They were known for throwing extravagant parties, but one night, they both disappeared. Some say they were murdered, others say it was something supernatural. No one really knows what happened, but their bodies were never found."

Tom whistled softly, glancing over at Ella. "And people still live there?"

"Not anymore," she replied. "It's been abandoned for decades. Now it's just a creepy old mansion that people dare each other to visit, especially around Halloween. Apparently, there've been lots of reports of strange noises, lights flickering, shadows moving—typical haunted house stuff."

Tom's grip on the steering wheel tightened just slightly. He wasn't superstitious, but there was something about the unknown that made him uneasy. Still, the idea of exploring a place with that kind of history was too intriguing to resist.

As they drove further out of the city, the streets grew quieter, and the houses became fewer and farther between. Soon, they were surrounded by dense woods on either side of the road, the darkness outside their windows interrupted only by the occasional passing car.

"Getting spooky already," Tom muttered, half-joking as they turned onto a gravel road that led to the mansion.

Ella smiled, her excitement undiminished. "Perfect, right? The isolation is part of the appeal."

A few minutes later, the mansion came into view. It stood at the top of a small hill, silhouetted against the night sky, its dark, towering shape looming over the landscape. The house itself was massive, with several tall, narrow windows, a wraparound porch, and a crumbling stone façade. Ivy crawled up the sides, giving it an even more eerie, abandoned look.

Tom pulled the car to a stop at the edge of the driveway, the gravel crunching under the tires. He turned off the engine and glanced over at Ella, whose wide smile hadn't faded.

"This is it," she said softly, her eyes fixed on the mansion. "The infamous haunted house."

Tom stared at the darkened windows, feeling a slight chill despite the warmth of the car. "You sure we're not trespassing?"

Ella shook her head. "I checked. It's open to the public—well, sort of. People are allowed to visit, but no one stays long. Apparently, the 'haunted' part keeps most people from wanting to explore too deeply."

Tom opened the car door, the cold night air rushing in as he stepped out. The mansion loomed before them, silent and still, its many windows staring down at them like eyes. The wind picked up, rustling the trees, and a faint creaking sound echoed from the porch.

"Ready?" Ella asked, stepping up beside him, her voice soft but full of excitement.

Tom nodded, though he couldn't shake the growing sense of unease. "Let's do this."

They made their way up the long, gravel path toward the house, their footsteps crunching loudly in the stillness of the night. The closer they got, the more imposing the mansion seemed. It was massive, its dark exterior blending into the night, and as they reached the front steps, Tom could see just how much the place had deteriorated over the years. The paint was peeling, and the wooden boards creaked ominously underfoot.

Ella reached for the brass doorknob, her hand hesitating for just a moment before she twisted it. The door swung open with an eerie creak, revealing a dark, cavernous hallway lit only by the faint glow of their flashlights.

"This is the part where people usually turn back," Ella whispered, her eyes wide with excitement.

Tom swallowed, stepping into the house behind her. The air inside was cold and musty, and the silence was oppressive, broken only by the distant sound of wind rattling through the old windows. The mansion's interior was as grand as its exterior, with a sweeping staircase in the center of the foyer and several arched doorways leading to other rooms.

They made their way through the house, their footsteps echoing loudly in the empty space. Every now and then, Tom caught a glimpse of something out of the corner of his eye—a flicker of movement, a shadow darting past—but when he turned to look, there was nothing there.

Ella, on the other hand, was completely fearless. She led the way through the mansion with an almost childlike sense of wonder, pointing out details of the house's architecture and speculating on what might have happened here all those years ago.

They wandered into what appeared to be a parlor, the room filled with dusty old furniture and a grand fireplace that hadn't been used in decades. Cobwebs clung to the corners, and the floor creaked with every step they took.

"This place must have been incredible back in the day," Ella said, her voice soft with awe. "Imagine the parties they must have had here."

Tom nodded, though his attention was focused on the strange feeling that had settled over him. It wasn't fear, exactly, but more like the sense of being watched. Every creak, every shift in the air felt like it was amplified by the silence, and the shadows seemed to move just out of reach of the flashlight's beam.

They continued through the house, exploring room after room, each one more eerie than the last. In the dining room, a long, dusty table was set with cracked plates and tarnished silverware, as though the owners had left in the middle of a meal and never returned. In the upstairs bedrooms, the old four-poster beds were draped in cobwebs, the curtains fluttering faintly in the draft.

At one point, as they were exploring a narrow hallway, Tom stopped suddenly, his breath catching in his throat. He had heard it—a faint whisper, like someone speaking just behind him. He turned quickly, shining his flashlight down the hall, but there was nothing there.

"Did you hear that?" he whispered, his voice barely audible.

Ella turned to him, her expression curious. "Hear what?"

Tom hesitated. "It sounded like... a whisper."

Ella's eyes gleamed with excitement, but she didn't seem alarmed. "Maybe the ghosts are saying hello."

Tom tried to laugh it off, but the unease stayed with him. As much as he wanted to enjoy the adventure, there was no denying that this place had an energy—something that made his skin prickle and his heart race.

After another hour of exploring, they finally made their way back to the front door. The wind had picked up outside, and as they stepped onto the porch, Tom let out a breath he hadn't realized he'd been holding.

"That was intense," he said, glancing back at the house.

Ella replied, her excitement still bubbling over. "I loved it. It's like stepping into another world."

Tom smiled, though the haunted feeling still lingered in his mind. As they walked back to the car, the mansion loomed behind them, its windows dark and watchful.

"Well," Tom said as they drove away, the mansion disappearing into the distance, "I can officially say I've visited a haunted house."

"And survived to tell the tale," Ella added with a grin.

Tom laughed, the tension finally easing. It had been a night of thrills and chills, but more than that, it had been another unforgettable adventure with Ella. One that left him both exhilarated and just a little spooked.

Chapter 11: The Halloween Bakery

The smell of cinnamon and sugar filled the air as Tom pushed open the door to the quaint bakery Ella had told him about. Located on a quiet corner of town, *Sweet Treats* had a reputation for its seasonal offerings, and in the weeks leading up to Halloween, the place transformed into a spooky wonderland of Halloween-themed pastries, cakes, and candies.

Tom had always had a sweet tooth, but when Ella suggested they spend the afternoon baking Halloween treats together, he realized this was about more than just desserts. It was about creating something together—about spending more time doing something simple yet meaningful.

Ella was already inside when he arrived, standing at the counter, admiring the selection of spooky treats on display. She looked up as the little bell above the door jingled, her face lighting up when she saw him.

"Hey! You made it," she called out, waving him over. "Look at these," she added, pointing to a tray of cupcakes decorated like little ghosts. "Aren't they adorable?"

Tom grinned as he joined her, his eyes scanning the display case. There were cupcakes with green frosting shaped like Frankenstein's monster, cookies cut out in the shapes of witches' hats and pumpkins, and even a row of mini pumpkin pies with perfectly browned crusts.

"This place is amazing," Tom said, feeling his mouth water just looking at the array of desserts.

Ella nodded enthusiastically. "I know, right? And we're going to make our own versions of these today."

Tom raised an eyebrow. "I didn't realize we were going pro with this baking thing."

Ella laughed, nudging him playfully. "Don't worry, I'll guide you through it. I've baked here a few times before, and they have everything you need. Plus, it's not just about making them perfect—it's about having fun."

Tom smiled at her infectious enthusiasm. He hadn't baked much in his life, but the idea of making Halloween treats with Ella sounded like a blast. It was a different kind of adventure—one that didn't involve haunted houses or costume parties, but something cozy and creative.

A few minutes later, they were led into the back of the bakery by one of the staff members, a friendly woman named Kate who ran the bakery's special "bake your own treats" workshop. The space was set up like a dream kitchen, with a large island counter, rows of baking supplies, and ovens along the walls. Bowls of colorful sprinkles, jars of candy eyes, and tubes of black and orange frosting sat waiting for them on the counter.

Ella rubbed her hands together excitedly. "Okay, first things first—cookies or cupcakes?"

Tom thought for a moment. "Let's start with cookies. I think I can handle that."

"Good choice," Ella said, pulling out a mixing bowl and handing it to him. "Let's get started."

Tom followed Ella's lead as she walked him through the process, starting with the basic cookie dough. She expertly measured the flour, sugar, and butter, explaining each step as she went. Tom did his best to keep up, but he couldn't help but get a little distracted watching how effortlessly Ella moved around the kitchen, her hands deftly working the ingredients into the perfect consistency.

"You're pretty good at this," Tom remarked, watching as she cracked an egg into the bowl with one hand.

Ella shrugged, a smile playing on her lips. "I've had a lot of practice. My mom and I used to bake together all the time. It was kind of our thing, especially around the holidays."

Tom nodded, feeling a warmth spread through him. "That's a nice tradition."

Ella glanced over at him, her smile softening. "Yeah, it is. I've always loved the holidays, but Halloween's definitely my favorite. There's just something about the creativity of it all—the decorations, the costumes, the treats. It's like you get to be a kid again, even as an adult."

Tom couldn't agree more. Ever since meeting Ella, he'd been feeling that sense of fun and magic that he hadn't experienced in years. Halloween had always been something he enjoyed, but this year, it felt different—more alive, more meaningful.

"Okay, dough's ready!" Ella declared, holding up the bowl triumphantly. "Now comes the fun part—shaping the cookies."

They rolled out the dough together, pressing cookie cutters shaped like bats, ghosts, and pumpkins into the soft dough. Tom's first few attempts were less than perfect, but Ella laughed good-naturedly as she helped him fix the edges of his misshapen cookies.

Once the cookies were cut and placed on the baking sheet, they popped them into the oven and turned their attention to the cupcakes. This time, Tom took the lead, following Ella's instructions as they mixed the batter. He added just a little extra pumpkin spice, grinning as Ella teased him for getting too enthusiastic with the spices.

"You're going to love them," he said confidently as he poured the batter into the cupcake liners.

Ella smirked. "We'll see. I'm reserving judgment until I taste one."

As they waited for the cookies and cupcakes to bake, they sat down at the counter, sipping on hot apple cider that the bakery provided for their workshop participants. The smell of cinnamon and sugar filled the room, and the warmth of the kitchen felt like the perfect escape from the chilly autumn air outside.

"I love this," Ella said softly, glancing around the bakery. "It's such a nice break from everything. Just... baking and relaxing."

Tom smiled, feeling the same sense of contentment. "Yeah, it's different from all the crazy Halloween stuff we've been doing, but it's nice. Feels... simple."

Ella nodded, her eyes warm. "Sometimes simple is the best."

They talked for a while longer, their conversation easy and flowing. Tom found himself opening up about things he didn't often talk about—his work, his family, and how he hadn't always made time for things like baking or holidays in recent years. Ella listened intently, sharing her own stories in return, and the more they talked, the more Tom realized how much he enjoyed these quiet moments with her.

After a while, the oven timer beeped, signaling that their cookies and cupcakes were ready. Ella jumped up, excited to see how everything had turned out. They carefully pulled the trays from the oven, setting them on the counter to cool.

The cookies had baked perfectly—golden brown around the edges, their spooky shapes still intact. The cupcakes, with their fragrant pumpkin spice scent, looked just as delicious, and Tom couldn't help but feel a little proud.

"Not bad for a first try," Ella said, grinning as she handed him a cookie cutter to start decorating.

Tom laughed. "I'll take it."

They spent the next hour decorating their creations, laughing as they added little candy eyes to the ghost-shaped cookies and piped orange and black frosting onto the cupcakes. Tom's decorating skills were questionable at best, but Ella's guidance made it fun, and by the end, they had a tray full of festive, if not slightly messy, Halloween treats.

Ella held up one of the cupcakes, inspecting it with a critical eye. "You know, your pumpkin spice additions actually worked. These taste amazing."

Tom grinned, biting into one of the cookies. "I told you. I'm secretly a baking genius."

They packed up their treats, ready to take them home and share with friends. But before they left, Ella turned to him, her face softening.

"I had a really good time today, Tom," she said quietly. "I'm glad we did this."

Tom smiled, his heart warm. "Me too. It was perfect."

Chapter 12: The Ghost Tour

The evening air was crisp, the scent of autumn leaves and distant wood smoke wafting through the streets as Tom and Ella made their way toward the meeting point for the city's famous ghost tour. Tom had always been a skeptic when it came to ghost stories, but when Ella suggested the tour, her eyes twinkling with excitement, he hadn't hesitated. How could he say no to another Halloween-themed adventure with her?

The city was alive with the spirit of the season. Jack-o'-lanterns flickered from the windows of old townhouses, and paper ghosts fluttered in the breeze, hung from trees lining the cobblestone streets. The sound of laughter and footsteps echoed around them as they reached the small park where the tour was set to begin.

A group had already gathered near the large stone fountain at the center of the park, and at the front of the group stood a tall man dressed in Victorian-era clothing, complete with a long black coat and a top hat. He held a lantern in one hand, its dim light casting flickering shadows on the ground, and in the other hand, he carried a book bound in cracked leather.

"That must be the guide," Ella whispered, nudging Tom as they joined the group.

"Looks like something out of a movie," Tom whispered back, unable to suppress a smile.

The guide, whose sharp features and piercing blue eyes added to his eerie appearance, stepped forward as the clock tower in the distance chimed seven. His voice, low and gravelly, immediately caught the group's attention.

"Welcome, brave souls, to the haunted heart of our city," he began, his voice echoing off the surrounding buildings. "Tonight, we will walk the very streets where the restless spirits of the past still linger, where tales of tragedy, mystery, and the supernatural have been whispered for centuries. But I must warn you—once we begin, there is no turning back."

Tom caught Ella's eye, and they exchanged amused smiles. The theatrics were a little over the top, but that was part of the fun.

The guide raised his lantern and motioned for the group to follow him. "Let us begin."

They made their way down the narrow streets, the soft glow of the streetlights casting long shadows across the cobblestones. The guide led them to the first stop on the tour—a centuries-old inn that had once been a popular stop for travelers in the 1800s but now stood empty and decrepit. Its windows were dark, and the building seemed to sag under the weight of its history.

The guide stopped in front of the inn, his voice dropping to a hushed tone. "This is where our first story begins. In 1852, this inn was the site of a terrible tragedy. A young woman, Mary Harper, was found dead in her room—her neck twisted, her face frozen in terror. Some say she was murdered by a jealous lover. Others believe something far more sinister took her life."

He paused, letting the words sink in. "To this day, guests who stay here report hearing her footsteps in the halls late at night. They feel a cold breath on the back of their necks, and some have even seen her reflection in the mirror, her eyes wide with fear."

Tom felt Ella shiver beside him, though she quickly tried to cover it up with a grin. "You okay?" he asked, his voice teasing.

Ella smirked. "Just getting into the spirit of things."

The guide continued the story, describing how no one had ever solved the mystery of Mary's death. Some believed the inn was cursed, others thought it was the work of an evil spirit. Either way, the inn had never been able to shake its reputation as one of the city's most haunted locations.

After a few more chilling details, the guide led them away from the inn and down a darkened alleyway. The cobblestones beneath their feet were slick with moisture, and the air seemed to grow colder as they ventured further into the narrow streets. Tom noticed that the other members of the group had fallen unusually quiet, their expressions ranging from intrigued to uneasy.

They arrived at the next stop—a grand old mansion that had once belonged to one of the city's wealthiest families. Its tall, iron gates stood open, and the front lawn was overgrown with weeds, giving it a desolate, forgotten feel. The guide stopped just outside the gates, raising his lantern to illuminate the mansion's façade.

"This," he said, his voice barely above a whisper, "is the Grayson House, home to one of the most famous ghost stories in the city."

Tom could sense Ella's excitement growing as the guide began to tell the story of the Grayson family—a family who had once been the toast of the city's elite. But their wealth had not protected them from tragedy. In the late 1800s, both Mr. and Mrs. Grayson died under mysterious circumstances, leaving their young daughter, Lillian, alone in the house. Lillian, devastated by the loss of her parents, was said to have slowly lost her mind. One night, she vanished, and though the police searched the house from top to bottom, she was never found.

"Some say Lillian's spirit still wanders these halls," the guide said, his voice low and eerie. "Visitors have reported hearing her laughter late at night, though no one has lived here for decades. Some have even seen her silhouette in the windows, watching and waiting."

Tom felt a chill run down his spine, and for a moment, he almost believed the story. There was something about the old mansion, standing silent and dark before them, that made it easy to imagine a ghostly figure lingering just beyond the windows.

Ella, however, was fully immersed in the tale, her eyes wide with fascination. "This place is incredible," she whispered. "I love how creepy it feels."

Tom chuckled softly. "It definitely has that haunted vibe."

They continued on the tour, stopping at various locations throughout the city, each with its own tragic tale of death, betrayal, or mysterious disappearances. The guide's voice never wavered, his stories spinning a web of fear and intrigue around the group, until even the skeptics seemed to be second-guessing the shadows that flickered in the corners of their vision.

The final stop on the tour brought them to a small cemetery at the edge of town, where the gravestones stood crooked and moss-covered, their inscriptions worn away by time. The guide led them through the gates, his lantern casting long, flickering shadows over the graves.

"This," he said, his voice barely above a whisper, "is where many of the city's most restless spirits are said to reside. Some of these souls met tragic ends, others lived long, bitter lives. But all of them share one thing in common—they have never truly left."

Tom glanced at Ella, who was standing quietly beside him, her eyes fixed on one of the gravestones. She seemed unusually still, her expression thoughtful.

"You okay?" he asked softly.

Ella nodded, but there was something in her voice that hinted at a deeper emotion. "It's just... cemeteries always make me think about life. How fragile it is. How easily it can slip away."

Tom reached out and gently squeezed her hand, feeling the warmth of her fingers in the cool night air. "Yeah, I know what you mean."

They stood there for a few moments longer, listening to the guide as he wrapped up the final story of the evening—a tale about a man who had been buried alive by mistake, his cries for help going unheard until it was too late.

By the time the tour ended, the group slowly began to disperse, some chatting quietly, others lost in thought. As Tom and Ella made their way back toward the center of town, the moon high overhead, Tom couldn't help but feel like the evening had brought them even closer. They had shared thrills and chills, but more than that, they had shared quiet moments of reflection, a sense of connection that went beyond the ghost stories.

As they reached the corner where their cars were parked, Ella turned to him, a small smile playing on her lips. "Thanks for coming with me tonight. I know ghost tours aren't really your thing."

Tom shrugged, his smile warm. "I had a great time. Besides, when you're with the right person, it doesn't matter what you're doing. It's always fun."

Ella's smile widened, and for a moment, they stood there in the glow of the streetlights, the world around them quiet and still.

"Next Halloween," she said softly, "we'll have to find an even scarier tour."

Tom laughed. "Deal."

Chapter 13: The Costume Competition

The local Halloween festival was in full swing when Tom and Ella arrived, their matching skeleton costumes glowing under the vibrant orange and purple lights that lit up the entire park. The air was thick with excitement as kids and adults alike wandered through the various booths, playing games, grabbing snacks, and showing off their costumes.

"Look at this place," Ella said, her eyes wide with wonder as they made their way through the crowd. "It's like Halloween exploded."

Tom nodded, grinning. "It's like every Halloween movie you've ever seen, all rolled into one."

They had been looking forward to this night for weeks. The festival had grown over the years, becoming one of the biggest Halloween events in the area, and this year's costume competition was rumored to be the most competitive yet. The streets were filled with people in elaborate outfits—pirates, witches, superheroes, and even a few creepy clowns wandering among the booths. The creativity and effort people put into their costumes were incredible, and Tom couldn't help but feel a surge of excitement as they approached the main stage where the contest would take place.

Tom and Ella had decided to enter as a couple. Their glowing skeleton costumes, which had been such a hit at Matt's Halloween party, seemed like the perfect choice. But this time, they had taken it up a notch. Ella had added intricate face paint to mimic skeletal features, with dark black eyes and white lines tracing down her cheekbones and jaw. Tom had followed her lead, and though his painting skills weren't as sharp as hers, Ella had helped fix his look, making sure they were perfectly matched.

"We're definitely going to stand out," Ella said confidently as they neared the registration table for the competition.

"Here's hoping," Tom replied, feeling a bit of competitive spirit rising. "Have you seen some of these costumes? I think we're going up against a whole team of zombies over there."

Ella glanced over at the group of people dressed in tattered clothing and realistic zombie makeup, their skin painted gray and bloodied. "Okay, yeah, they're good. But I think we've got an edge."

Tom grinned. "What's that?"

"Style," Ella said, winking. "And we glow in the dark."

They signed up for the competition, getting their number—#21—and mingled with the other contestants while they waited for the judging to begin. The stage was set up with dramatic Halloween decorations—glowing pumpkins, fog machines, and eerie music playing in the background. As they walked around, Tom noticed a couple dressed as famous movie characters—one was dressed as Frankenstein, complete with a greenish tint to his skin and bolts protruding from his neck, while the other was dressed as the Bride of Frankenstein, her dark hair styled in an intricate updo.

Ella nudged Tom, her eyes widening. "Okay, now that's impressive."

Tom nodded, feeling a flicker of doubt. "Yeah... maybe we should've gone with something more elaborate."

Ella shook her head, her expression firm. "No way. We've got this. Besides, it's not just about the costume. It's about the attitude."

Tom smiled at her confidence. She was right. Halloween wasn't about perfection—it was about fun, creativity, and standing out in your own way. And that's what they'd done. Their costumes were simple, but they were bold, and the fact that they glowed in the dark made them even more striking.

"Alright," Tom said, feeling his confidence return. "Let's show them what we've got."

As they waited for their turn, they watched the other contestants take the stage one by one. There were a few showstoppers—the zombies, the Frankenstein couple, and a group dressed as classic movie monsters, complete with a werewolf, a mummy, and Dracula. The judges, a panel of local artists and festival organizers, seemed impressed, and the crowd cheered loudly for each group.

Finally, it was their turn. The announcer called their number, and Ella gave Tom's hand a quick squeeze before they walked toward the stage.

"And next up, we have contestant number 21!" the announcer's voice boomed through the speakers. "Tom and Ella, dressed as... glowing skeletons!"

The crowd clapped and cheered as they stepped onto the stage. The bright lights hit them, but once the stage lighting dimmed slightly, the real magic of their costumes came to life. Under the blacklights, the glow-in-the-dark bones on their outfits lit up brilliantly, and the audience let out a collective "ooh" as they saw the full effect.

Ella leaned in close to Tom and whispered, "Ready to do a little skeleton dance?"

Tom chuckled. "Let's do it."

With that, they began to move in sync, swaying their arms and legs in a mock skeleton dance that Ella had taught Tom earlier in the week. It was goofy and lighthearted, and the crowd loved it, laughing and cheering as they performed their silly moves on stage. Their costumes glowed, their faces painted in intricate skeletal designs, and they danced around like they were having the time of their lives.

Tom couldn't stop smiling. He had never thought of himself as someone who would get up on a stage and perform, but with Ella by his side, it was easy to let loose and enjoy the moment. The audience's energy was infectious, and by the time they finished their little routine, Tom could feel the adrenaline pumping.

They took a bow as the crowd cheered loudly, and the announcer laughed into the microphone. "Now that's what I call getting into the Halloween spirit! Great job, Tom and Ella!"

They walked off the stage, laughing and catching their breath. "I think we nailed it," Ella said, her eyes gleaming with excitement.

Tom nodded, still smiling. "We definitely had fun."

As the rest of the contestants finished their performances, the judges gathered to deliberate. Tom and Ella stood with the other participants, waiting for the results. The crowd buzzed with anticipation, and Tom could feel the excitement building around them. He glanced over at Ella, who was grinning from ear to ear, her eyes still sparkling with that Halloween magic.

Finally, the announcer returned to the stage, microphone in hand. "Alright, everyone! The judges have made their decision, and it's time to announce the winners of this year's costume competition!"

The crowd erupted into cheers, and the announcer began to list the awards. First came the prize for the best group costume, which went to the classic movie monsters. Next was the best individual costume, awarded to a young girl dressed as an impressively detailed, life-sized doll. The crowd clapped enthusiastically for each winner, and Tom felt his heart pound in his chest as they neared the announcement for best couple's costume.

"And now," the announcer continued, drawing out the suspense, "for the best couple's costume, the winners are…"

Tom held his breath, glancing over at Ella.

"Tom and Ella, the glowing skeletons!"

The crowd roared with approval, and Tom felt a surge of joy as he and Ella were called up to the stage. They walked up together, hand in hand, beaming as they accepted their prize—an oversized Halloween trophy adorned with a grinning jack-o'-lantern.

Chapter 14: The Pumpkin Carving Contest

A crisp autumn breeze rustled through the trees as Tom and Ella made their way toward the town's annual pumpkin carving contest. The event was held in the town square, and as they approached, Tom could see the familiar rows of tables already set up, each one adorned with orange pumpkins of all shapes and sizes.

The air was filled with the scent of spiced apple cider and warm pumpkin treats from the nearby food stalls, and the chatter of excited participants filled the square. Laughter and conversation floated through the air as families, friends, and couples picked out their pumpkins and began preparing for the competition.

"This is it," Ella said with a grin, her eyes gleaming as they approached the registration table. "Time to show off our carving skills."

Tom chuckled, glancing around at the pumpkins already on display. Some people had carved intricate designs in previous years, with everything from spooky haunted houses to elaborate scenes of Halloween night. He couldn't help but feel a flicker of doubt. Carving a pumpkin had always been a fun tradition, but he'd never considered himself much of an artist.

"Let's just hope I don't mess up and turn my pumpkin into a pile of mush," Tom said, half-joking as they signed their names for the contest.

Ella laughed softly, nudging him with her elbow. "You'll do great. Besides, this is about having fun. No pressure."

She smiled reassuringly as they moved over to one of the long tables, which was covered with all the tools they'd need: carving knives, scoops, and stencils for those who wanted a little extra help with their designs. Tom and Ella both grabbed a pumpkin from the nearby display, settling on two that were roughly the same size and shape.

As they sat down, Tom studied his pumpkin for a moment, wondering what kind of design he should go for. Something simple, he decided—probably a classic jack-o'-lantern face with triangle eyes and a toothy grin.

"Do you have a plan?" Tom asked, glancing at Ella, who was already starting to draw her design on her pumpkin with a marker.

Ella nodded, a grin spreading across her face. "I think I'm going for a spooky spider web with a little spider in the corner."

Tom raised an eyebrow, impressed. "That's pretty ambitious."

Ella shrugged playfully. "I like to challenge myself. Plus, it'll be fun."

Tom shook his head, smiling as he picked up his carving tools. "I'm sticking with something more traditional. Classic jack-o'-lantern."

"That's a solid choice," Ella said, glancing over at him as she worked on her design. "Nothing wrong with a classic."

The sound of scraping pumpkin guts filled the air as the contestants got to work, the atmosphere around them buzzing with excitement. Tom found himself getting lost in the process—scooping out the insides of the pumpkin, carefully sketching out his design, and finally making the first cut. As he carved, he realized how calming the activity was. It was easy to forget about everything else and focus on creating something fun, even if it wasn't the most artistic.

After a while, Ella glanced over at him, her eyes bright with amusement. "How's it going over there?"

Tom smiled, holding up his half-finished pumpkin for her to see. "Not too bad. I've got the eyes and mouth down, just need to finish the teeth."

Ella grinned, leaning closer to inspect it. "I like it. It's got that perfect mix of creepy and cute."

Tom laughed. "That's exactly what I was going for."

He watched as Ella continued carving her own pumpkin, her hands moving with a kind of grace that made it clear she had done this before. The spider web design was starting to take shape, with delicate lines forming the web across the front of the pumpkin, and a small spider dangling from one corner. It was intricate and impressive, and Tom couldn't help but admire how effortlessly she made it look.

"You're really good at this," Tom said, shaking his head in awe. "I think we've got a winner right here."

Ella shrugged, her cheeks flushing slightly at the compliment. "It's just practice. My mom and I used to carve pumpkins every year when I was a kid. We'd spend hours coming up with new designs."

Tom nodded, understanding the sentiment. "We used to do it every year too, but I think my designs peaked when I was about ten."

Ella laughed softly. "Well, it's like riding a bike. You never forget how to make a good jack-o'-lantern."

As they continued working on their pumpkins, Tom couldn't help but feel a sense of contentment settle over him. This Halloween had been more than just a series of fun events—it had been an opportunity to connect with Ella in ways he hadn't expected. Every adventure, every moment they spent together felt like it was deepening their bond, and he couldn't help but wonder where it might lead.

After another half hour of carving, they both set down their tools, admiring their finished pumpkins. Tom's jack-o'-lantern had turned out better than expected, with a wide, toothy grin and jagged eyes that gave it a mischievous look. Ella's pumpkin, on the other hand, was a work of art. The spider web design was flawless, and the little spider dangling in the corner looked almost lifelike.

"I think we've outdone ourselves," Ella said, beaming as she held up her pumpkin. "I'm really proud of how this one turned out."

Tom nodded, feeling proud of his own creation as well. "We make a pretty good team."

As they placed their pumpkins on the judging table with the others, Tom couldn't help but feel a rush of excitement. The competition was stiff, with plenty of creative and well-executed designs, but he was proud of what they had accomplished. It wasn't about winning—it was about the fun they had along the way.

The judges, a mix of local artists and town officials, began walking up and down the row of pumpkins, inspecting each one carefully. Tom and Ella watched from a distance, holding hands as they waited for the results.

"Do you think we have a chance?" Tom asked, glancing at Ella.

Ella smiled, her confidence never wavering. "I think we did great. But even if we don't win, this was so much fun. That's what matters."

Tom nodded, feeling the same. The whole experience had been a blast, and the joy of spending time with Ella was worth more than any prize.

After what felt like forever, the head judge stepped up to the microphone, a small smile on her face. "Thank you all for participating in this year's pumpkin carving contest! We've seen some truly incredible designs tonight, and it was tough to choose, but we have our winners."

The crowd quieted as the judge began announcing the winners, starting with the categories for "Best Traditional Design" and "Most Creative Use of a Pumpkin." Tom and Ella listened intently, waiting to hear if their names would be called.

"And now," the judge said, glancing down at her notes, "the winner for 'Best Overall Design' is... Ella and her spooky spider web!"

Ella's face lit up with surprise, her eyes wide as the crowd clapped and cheered. She turned to Tom, laughing in disbelief. "I can't believe it!"

They made their way to the front, where Ella accepted the small trophy and a basket filled with Halloween-themed goodies. She beamed as they took a picture with her winning pumpkin, and as they walked back to their table, Ella turned to Tom, her smile softening.

"This was perfect," she said quietly. "Thank you for doing this with me."

Tom squeezed her hand, feeling a warmth spread through him. "I wouldn't have missed it for the world."

Chapter 15: The Halloween Maze Adventure

Tom and Ella made their way toward the entrance of the Halloween corn maze. It had been one of the last-minute additions to their Halloween adventure list, but Ella had insisted they try it. "What's Halloween without getting lost in a spooky maze?" she'd said with a grin, and Tom hadn't needed much convincing.

The maze was part of a local farm's annual Halloween festivities, and as they approached, they could hear the distant sound of laughter and the faint screams of those already wandering through the winding paths. String lights hung overhead, casting a soft orange glow over the entrance, and a sign nearby read: *Welcome to the Maze of Terror. Enter if you dare!*

Tom chuckled at the dramatic sign as they reached the entrance. "Maze of terror, huh? How scary can it really be?"

Ella raised an eyebrow, her grin mischievous. "You never know. These places can get pretty creative with their scares."

Tom wasn't so sure. He'd never been one to scare easily, but he loved that Ella was always game for anything that added a little thrill to their Halloween adventures. And he had to admit, there was something about walking into a maze in the dark that made his pulse quicken a little.

They bought their tickets and made their way toward the entrance. A man dressed as a scarecrow stood at the gate, his painted face eerie in the flickering light. He tipped his straw hat at them, his voice low and ominous. "Beware what lies within. Many have entered, but few find their way out without a fright."

Tom smirked, but Ella played along, pretending to shiver dramatically. "Spooky," she whispered, leaning closer to Tom as they passed the scarecrow.

"Very," Tom replied with a grin, though his excitement was starting to build. There was something about the atmosphere—the cool air, the distant sounds of other people lost in the maze, the glow of the orange lights—that made him feel like anything could happen.

They stepped into the maze, and the tall corn stalks closed in around them, blocking out much of the outside world. The path before them twisted and turned, narrow and uneven, and the moonlight overhead barely filtered through the dense growth. For a moment, it felt as if they had entered another world entirely—a world of mystery, shadows, and the unknown.

Ella looked around, her eyes sparkling with excitement. "Okay, so which way do we go?"

Tom shrugged, glancing down both directions of the path before them. "Left?"

"Left it is," Ella said with a grin, taking his hand as they started down the path.

The maze was eerily quiet at first, the only sounds coming from the rustling of the corn and the occasional distant voice. As they walked, Tom noticed how disorienting it was—each turn looked the same, and the tall corn stalks loomed over them, making it difficult to get any sense of direction. But that was part of the fun, he realized. It wasn't just about the scare—it was about the thrill of being lost, of not knowing what might be around the next corner.

They wandered deeper into the maze, taking random turns and laughing whenever they hit a dead end. Each time they found themselves backtracking, Ella would tease Tom about his sense of direction, though neither of them was particularly bothered by the idea of being lost for a while. It was all part of the adventure.

After about fifteen minutes of wandering, they turned a corner and came face to face with their first scare—a life-sized, animatronic witch perched on a crooked broomstick. Her green face was twisted into a wicked grin, and as they passed, she cackled loudly, her glowing red eyes following them.

Ella jumped slightly, laughing as she clutched Tom's arm. "Okay, that got me!"

Tom chuckled, shaking his head. "I wasn't expecting that, either."

The scares became more frequent as they ventured deeper into the maze. A creepy clown jumped out from behind a stack of hay bales, making Ella shriek and then laugh. A man dressed as a zombie stumbled across their path, moaning and dragging his feet, his costume impressively detailed with fake blood and torn clothing. Despite the jumps, neither of them felt genuinely scared—just thrilled by the fun of it all.

"This is great," Ella said, her laughter filling the air as they walked away from yet another spooky scare—a fog machine spewing mist into the air as eerie music played from hidden speakers. "It's like we're kids again, just running around, getting spooked."

Tom nodded, his heart light. He was having the time of his life. There was something freeing about letting go, allowing himself to get swept up in the silliness of it all. It was another reminder of how much he loved spending time with Ella—how every moment with her, whether they were carving pumpkins or navigating a maze, felt like an adventure.

After a while, they hit another dead end, and Ella stopped, looking around with a playful frown. "Okay, I admit it—I have no idea where we are."

Tom laughed, glancing around. "Should we try backtracking?"

"Maybe," Ella said, though her smile told him she wasn't in any hurry to get out. "Unless you have some kind of secret maze skills you've been hiding?"

"Not exactly," Tom admitted, glancing down the path they had come from. "But I'm willing to guess our way out."

They turned around and began retracing their steps, but before they could get far, the sound of footsteps behind them made Tom stop. He turned, his eyes narrowing as he peered through the corn. For a moment, all he saw was darkness—but then, a tall figure emerged from the shadows.

It was a man dressed in a tattered black cloak, his face hidden behind a grotesque skull mask. He held a rusty scythe in one hand, its blade glinting in the moonlight, and as he approached, he raised the scythe over his head, letting out a low, guttural growl.

Ella gasped, gripping Tom's arm as they both stared at the figure.

"Uh... time to go?" Tom suggested, already backing away.

"Time to go!" Ella agreed, laughing as she tugged him down the path.

They took off, laughing and dodging through the maze as the figure in the cloak followed them, his heavy footsteps echoing in the night. Tom wasn't sure how long the chase lasted, but it was exhilarating—their laughter mixing with the thrill of being pursued, the adrenaline of not knowing what was around each corner.

Eventually, they lost sight of the figure, and they stopped to catch their breath, leaning against the wooden posts marking one of the paths.

"That was awesome," Ella panted, still laughing as she wiped the sweat from her brow. "I think that might have been the best scare of the night."

Tom grinned, his heart still racing. "Definitely. I didn't know we were getting a full workout with this maze."

They stood there for a moment, catching their breath and exchanging grins. Then Ella glanced around, her expression turning mock-serious. "Okay, now we really have no idea where we are."

Tom chuckled. "True, but we'll find our way out eventually."

With renewed determination, they set off again, taking a few wrong turns before finally stumbling upon the exit. As they stepped out of the maze, a cheer went up from the staff members standing by the entrance, congratulating them on making it through.

Ella beamed, her face flushed with excitement. "We survived the maze of terror!"

Tom laughed, his own excitement bubbling over. "Barely!"

Chapter 16: The Midnight Cemetery Visit

The clock struck midnight, and the quiet streets of the town lay shrouded in an eerie mist. Tom and Ella stood at the gates of the old cemetery, their breath visible in the cool October air. The tall, wrought-iron gate before them creaked in the wind, and the shadows cast by the moonlight gave the gravestones inside an otherworldly glow.

Ella adjusted her jacket and shot Tom a playful grin. "Are you ready for this?"

Tom raised an eyebrow, glancing at the cemetery beyond the gate. "Midnight in a cemetery? Seems like the perfect place for a horror movie, but yeah, I'm ready."

This midnight visit to the cemetery had been Ella's idea, naturally. It was one of the last things on their Halloween adventure list, and Ella had insisted that they visit the cemetery at the witching hour, when legend said the spirits were most active.

The cemetery was one of the oldest in town, dating back to the 1800s. Its headstones were weathered and cracked, some tilted from years of neglect. The place had always given off an eerie vibe, even during the day, but at night, with only the faint light of the moon and stars to guide them, it felt like they were stepping into another world.

Tom pushed open the gate, its hinges groaning as it swung inward. The sound echoed through the still night, amplifying the sense that they were trespassing on something ancient and forgotten.

"Well, here we go," Tom said, glancing back at Ella as she followed him inside.

They walked down the narrow gravel path that wound through the cemetery, their footsteps crunching softly. The wind rustled the leaves on the ground, and the air was thick with the scent of damp earth and decaying foliage. Tom couldn't help but feel a chill crawl down his spine, though whether it was from the cold or the atmosphere, he couldn't be sure.

"Do you ever wonder what it's like for the people buried here?" Ella asked quietly, her voice soft in the stillness. "Like, what their lives were like before all this?"

Tom glanced around at the rows of headstones, the names barely visible in the dim light. "Yeah, I guess so. It's strange to think about all the stories that must be buried here."

Ella nodded, her eyes scanning the graves. "I've always found cemeteries fascinating. They're peaceful, but there's this sense of history—like you're walking among ghosts."

Tom chuckled, though he understood what she meant. There was something about a cemetery, especially at night, that made you think about life and death in a different way. It was both peaceful and eerie, a reminder of how fleeting everything was.

They wandered deeper into the cemetery, their conversation falling into a comfortable silence. The air seemed to grow colder as they walked, and Tom noticed that the mist had thickened, swirling around their feet like ghostly fingers. Every now and then, the wind would pick up, making the trees creak and groan, and Tom couldn't help but glance over his shoulder, half-expecting to see something moving in the shadows.

"This is definitely spooky," Tom admitted, his voice low.

Ella smiled, her eyes glinting in the moonlight. "That's the point. There's something thrilling about being somewhere like this at midnight. It's like... you're tempting fate."

They reached a small hill at the center of the cemetery, where a large, crumbling mausoleum stood. The stone structure was covered in ivy, its entrance sealed by a rusty iron gate. Ella stopped in front of it, staring at the inscription carved into the stone above the doorway.

"'The Beckett Family, 1879,'" Ella read aloud. "I remember hearing about them. They were one of the wealthiest families in town back in the day."

Tom nodded. "Didn't something tragic happen to them?"

Ella's smile faded slightly as she nodded. "Yeah. Apparently, the whole family died under mysterious circumstances. No one ever figured out what happened. Some say it was an illness, others say it was a curse."

Tom raised an eyebrow, glancing at the darkened entrance of the mausoleum. "A curse?"

Ella shrugged. "It's just one of the stories people tell. But you know how small towns are—every old family has some kind of creepy legend attached to them."

Tom leaned against a nearby headstone, staring up at the mausoleum. The wind picked up again, making the leaves on the trees rustle and swirl in the air. For a moment, it felt as though the whole cemetery was holding its breath, waiting for something.

"Do you believe in ghosts?" Ella asked suddenly, breaking the silence.

Tom thought for a moment, glancing over at her. "I don't know. I've never seen one, but... I guess it's possible."

Ella nodded thoughtfully, her gaze fixed on the mausoleum. "I've always been fascinated by the idea of spirits. I don't know if I believe in them, but the idea that people might leave something behind, that part of them stays connected to the world—it's kind of beautiful, in a strange way."

Tom smiled, watching her as she spoke. He loved the way Ella saw the world, the way she found meaning and beauty in things most people overlooked. Even in a place like this, in the middle of the night, she found a way to make it feel more than just spooky—she made it feel like an adventure, like there was something deeper waiting to be discovered.

They stood there for a while, staring up at the mausoleum, lost in their own thoughts. The night was so still, so quiet, that Tom could hear his own breathing, the sound of the wind in the trees, and the occasional distant cry of an owl.

"I wonder what they'd think," Ella said softly, "if they knew people were still visiting their graves, still talking about them."

Tom chuckled. "They'd probably think we're crazy."

Ella grinned. "Probably."

They continued walking, weaving through the rows of graves and reading the names and dates etched into the stones. Some of the graves were over a hundred years old, the inscriptions worn away by time, while others were newer, marked by fresh flowers left by loved ones.

As they neared the edge of the cemetery, Tom spotted a tall statue—a stone angel with its wings outstretched, standing watch over a cluster of graves. Its face was serene, its hands clasped in prayer, and for a moment, Tom felt a strange sense of peace wash over him. The angel seemed to glow in the moonlight, its presence both calming and otherworldly.

Ella followed his gaze, her expression softening. "I love that statue," she said quietly. "It's like a guardian for the people buried here."

Tom nodded, feeling the same. There was something comforting about the angel, a sense that even in a place like this, there was still hope, still light.

They stood there for a few more minutes, watching the angel as the wind whispered through the trees. It was peaceful, almost tranquil, and Tom found himself forgetting about the spookiness of the cemetery. Instead, he felt connected to the place in a way he hadn't expected—as if the cemetery wasn't just a place for the dead, but a reminder of the stories that lived on, even after people were gone.

As they finally made their way back toward the gate, the night still dark and quiet around them, Ella took Tom's hand, her fingers warm against his in the cool air.

"Thanks for coming with me tonight," she said softly. "I know this wasn't your usual kind of adventure."

Tom smiled, squeezing her hand. "I'm glad we did it. It was... different. In a good way."

Chapter 17: Halloween Traditions Revealed

Tom and Ella made their way back to his apartment after spending the day in town. Halloween was just a few days away, and the excitement was building in the air. Kids were already running through the streets, their voices carrying with the wind as they discussed their upcoming costumes and Halloween plans.

"Can you believe Halloween is almost here?" Ella asked, her voice filled with excitement as she held Tom's hand. "It feels like this month flew by."

Tom nodded, glancing at her with a smile. "Yeah, it's been non-stop, but I wouldn't have it any other way. It's been pretty perfect."

Ella smiled, her eyes softening. "It has, hasn't it?"

They had done everything from pumpkin carving contests to haunted hayrides, and each experience had brought them closer together. As they strolled through the streets, the cool autumn breeze rustling through the trees, Tom couldn't help but feel that Halloween had become more than just a holiday for them—it had turned into a season of memories, a time when they got to share little pieces of their past and build something together.

As they stepped into Tom's apartment, the warm, familiar smell of cinnamon and cloves greeted them. Tom had lit one of his favorite fall candles earlier, filling the space with a cozy, inviting atmosphere. Ella immediately made her way over to the couch, sinking into it with a contented sigh.

"I think this is the first time we've had a night to just relax in weeks," she said, laughing softly. "I almost forgot what it feels like."

Tom chuckled, sitting down beside her. "Yeah, we've definitely been busy. But it's been worth it."

Ella smiled, leaning back against the cushions. "It has. I can't believe how much we've done this month. It's been like one long Halloween adventure."

Tom nodded, feeling the same. There had been something magical about every moment they had spent together, and as Halloween approached, he couldn't help but wonder how they might keep that magic going beyond the holiday.

"So," Tom said, glancing at her playfully. "I've been meaning to ask—what are your Halloween traditions? I mean, beyond all the fun stuff we've done this year. What do you usually do when it's just you?"

Ella thought for a moment, her eyes brightening with a smile. "Well, I've always had a few things I do every year. Growing up, Halloween was a big deal in my house. My mom would start decorating at the beginning of October—she'd go all out, like we've been doing this year, but even crazier. We'd carve pumpkins, make spooky treats, and have a big movie night on Halloween itself."

Tom smiled, imagining a younger Ella running around her house, helping her mom decorate. "That sounds amazing."

Ella nodded, her expression softening with nostalgia. "It was. We always had this big Halloween dinner, too. My mom would make pumpkin soup and these little ghost-shaped sandwiches. It was silly, but I loved it. Then, after dinner, we'd settle in and watch movies—usually something classic like *Hocus Pocus* or *Beetlejuice*. That was the part I looked forward to the most."

Tom could hear the warmth in her voice as she talked about her childhood traditions. "So, do you still do the big dinner and movie night?"

Ella shrugged. "I've tried to keep some of it going, but it's been different since I moved here. It's hard to recreate all those things on your own, you know? But I always make time for a movie marathon on Halloween night. That's one tradition I've held on to."

Tom nodded thoughtfully, understanding how hard it must have been to let go of some of those childhood traditions. But he could also hear how much they meant to her, and he wanted to help her hold on to those memories in some way.

"I think we should do the movie marathon," Tom suggested. "You, me, some spooky snacks—let's bring that tradition back."

Ella's face lit up with a wide smile. "Really? You'd want to do that?"

"Absolutely," Tom said, his voice sincere. "I mean, we've already done so much Halloween stuff together. It feels like the perfect way to wrap up the month. And besides, I'm always down for a good movie marathon."

Ella laughed, nodding enthusiastically. "Okay, it's a deal. But we have to go all out—candles, blankets, snacks. I want to do it right."

Tom grinned, loving her energy. "We'll do it right."

They sat there for a while, talking about their favorite Halloween movies, discussing which ones they should watch for their marathon. Ella's enthusiasm was contagious, and Tom found himself looking forward to the idea of a quiet, cozy Halloween night with her.

After a few minutes, Ella turned to him, her eyes thoughtful. "What about you?" she asked. "What are your Halloween traditions?"

Tom paused, considering the question. "Well, it wasn't as big of a deal in my house growing up," he admitted. "We did the usual stuff—trick-or-treating, pumpkin carving. But as I got older, I sort of drifted away from it. I think that's why this year has been so special. I haven't done this much for Halloween in a long time."

Ella smiled, her expression softening. "I'm glad you've had fun."

"I really have," Tom said, his voice sincere. "It's been incredible—better than any Halloween I've had in years. And I think it's because I've been doing all of it with you."

Ella's cheeks flushed slightly, her smile growing. "I feel the same way. This year has been... different. In the best way."

They sat there for a moment, their hands intertwined, the quiet of the room wrapping around them like a warm blanket. Tom felt a sense of peace settle over him, and as he looked into Ella's eyes, he realized that this Halloween wasn't just about the fun, spooky things they had done together—it was about the connection they had built, the moments they had shared that went beyond the decorations and the costumes.

"So," Ella said, breaking the silence with a playful grin. "Are we adding any new traditions this year?"

Tom raised an eyebrow, intrigued. "New traditions? Like what?"

Ella leaned closer, her voice teasing. "I don't know. Maybe something a little more adventurous? Maybe we come up with a crazy Halloween challenge every year. Something that pushes us out of our comfort zone—like visiting the scariest haunted house in the state, or creating the most over-the-top costumes we can think of."

Tom laughed, loving the idea. "I'm in. Let's make it a tradition."

Ella smiled, her eyes glinting with excitement. "Good. Because I have a feeling next year is going to be even better."

Chapter 18: The Fortune Teller's Prediction

The small, dimly lit tent stood at the edge of the Halloween festival, its entrance draped in heavy black and purple velvet curtains. A sign outside read, *Madame Zara: Fortune Teller, Tarot Reader, and Seer of All Futures.* Flickering candles cast long shadows, making the whole setup feel mysterious and otherworldly, and Tom could already hear the soft tinkling of wind chimes coming from inside.

Tom glanced over at Ella, whose eyes were wide with excitement as they approached the tent. "Are you sure you want to do this?" he asked with a grin. "You know, fortune tellers can be... unpredictable."

Ella laughed, nudging him playfully. "That's the point! It's fun, and besides, who wouldn't want to know their future?"

Tom chuckled. He wasn't sure he believed in fortune telling or tarot readings, but there was something about the allure of the mysterious that intrigued him. He could see that Ella was eager to go through with it, and frankly, he was curious too.

They had been wandering around the festival, enjoying the sights and sounds of the final night before Halloween. The whole place was alive with energy—booths selling candy apples and caramel popcorn, kids in costumes running around, and street performers putting on spooky shows. But when they passed the fortune teller's tent, Ella had stopped in her tracks, clearly unable to resist the pull of the unknown.

"I'm in," Tom said, grinning as they reached the entrance of the tent. "Let's see what the future holds."

Ella smiled brightly and stepped inside first, holding the curtain open for him to follow. The inside of the tent was even darker than the outside. It smelled of incense and something sweet, like vanilla or cinnamon. Heavy tapestries lined the walls, and the small space was illuminated only by the glow of a few candles placed on a round table in the center of the room. The table was covered with a deep purple cloth, and sitting behind it was Madame Zara herself.

The fortune teller was an older woman with long, flowing silver hair, wearing an array of necklaces and bracelets that jingled softly as she moved. Her eyes were lined with kohl, giving her a mysterious, almost ethereal appearance. She glanced up as Tom and Ella entered, her sharp eyes studying them carefully before she smiled.

"Welcome," she said in a low, velvety voice. "I've been expecting you."

Ella exchanged a wide-eyed look with Tom before stepping closer to the table. "You have?" she asked, her tone half-joking, half-serious.

Madame Zara nodded slowly, her gaze never leaving them. "The spirits told me two curious souls would visit tonight, seeking answers they do not yet know they need."

Tom raised an eyebrow, suppressing a smile. He wasn't sure if Madame Zara was playing into the theatrics of it all, but it was definitely entertaining.

"Please," Madame Zara continued, gesturing to the two chairs in front of her. "Sit. Let us see what the cards reveal."

Tom and Ella exchanged glances and then sat down across from the fortune teller. The air inside the tent felt heavy, as if the outside world had vanished, leaving only this small, dimly lit space where time seemed to stand still.

Madame Zara reached for a worn deck of tarot cards on the table and began to shuffle them with slow, deliberate movements. The cards made a soft, shuffling sound as they slid through her fingers, and Tom felt a strange sense of anticipation building inside him. He wasn't sure why—it wasn't like he actually believed in this—but there was something about the moment, the way the atmosphere seemed to shift, that made him curious.

Ella, sitting beside him, was practically buzzing with excitement. Her eyes were fixed on Madame Zara's hands, and Tom could tell she was completely enthralled by the experience.

Madame Zara shuffled the deck one last time before placing it in front of them. "Cut the deck," she instructed, her voice soft but firm.

Ella reached out and carefully cut the deck into two piles. Madame Zara nodded approvingly and began to deal the cards onto the table, laying them out in a pattern that Tom vaguely recognized from movies and books—a cross shape with a few additional cards around the edges.

Once the cards were laid out, Madame Zara sat back slightly, her gaze sweeping over them. For a long moment, she didn't speak, her eyes narrowing as if she were studying the cards intently. Tom felt the tension build in the room, the air growing heavier with each passing second.

Finally, she looked up at Tom and Ella, her voice low and filled with meaning. "The two of you are bound together by something powerful," she said, her words slow and deliberate. "I see a connection—strong, unbreakable. You have shared much, and you will continue to share even more."

Tom exchanged a glance with Ella, who was watching the fortune teller with rapt attention.

Madame Zara continued, her finger lightly tracing over one of the cards. "But I also see challenges ahead. There will be moments of uncertainty, moments where you will have to trust in each other fully. The road ahead will not always be easy, but together, you will find your way."

Tom's heart quickened slightly at her words, though he wasn't sure why. It was vague, but there was something about the way she said it, as if she knew more than she was letting on.

"And here," Madame Zara said, tapping a card at the center of the spread. "This card represents your future. There is great potential, a deep love that can grow stronger with time. But…" she paused, her eyes narrowing slightly as she studied the card.

Ella leaned forward, her voice barely above a whisper. "But what?"

Madame Zara's gaze flicked to Ella. "But you must be careful not to let fear stand in your way. The fear of what-ifs, of the unknown—it can be your greatest enemy. But if you face it together, there is nothing you cannot overcome."

Tom felt a lump form in his throat as he listened. Part of him knew it was just a performance, just the fortune teller weaving a story, but another part of him—deeper, more vulnerable—couldn't help but feel the weight of her words.

Madame Zara leaned back, her gaze softening as she looked at them. "Remember," she said quietly, "the future is not set in stone. It is shaped by the choices you make, the risks you take, and the love you give."

Tom and Ella sat in silence for a moment, absorbing her words. Finally, Madame Zara gathered the cards and placed them back in the deck, her movements slow and deliberate.

"Thank you," Ella said softly, her voice filled with wonder. "That was… incredible."

Madame Zara smiled, her eyes twinkling. "Go forth with an open heart, and the future will be kind to you."

"What do you think?" Ella asked, her voice bright with curiosity. "Do you think she was right?"

Tom smiled, glancing over at her. "I don't know. But I do know that no matter what happens, we've got this."

Chapter 19: Halloween at Home

Halloween night had finally arrived, and for the first time in weeks, Tom and Ella had no big plans. No costume parties, no haunted hayrides, no pumpkin carving contests. Instead, they had decided to spend Halloween at home—a quiet night filled with snacks, movies, and the simple joy of each other's company.

Tom stood in the kitchen, stirring a pot of pumpkin soup while the smell of spiced cider simmering on the stove filled the apartment. The soft glow of candlelight flickered on the counter, casting a warm, cozy ambiance over the room. Outside, the wind rattled the windows, and Tom could hear the faint sound of children laughing as they trick-or-treated down the street.

Ella was in the living room, busy setting up their Halloween movie marathon. She had insisted on keeping things simple for their night in, but she hadn't skimped on the details. The couch was piled with blankets and pillows, and the coffee table was laden with bowls of popcorn, candy corn, and the ghost-shaped cookies they had baked earlier in the day. A stack of Halloween classics sat next to the TV—*Hocus Pocus*, *The Nightmare Before Christmas*, and *Beetlejuice* among them.

Tom smiled to himself as he ladled the soup into two bowls, carefully balancing them on a tray along with the cider. This night was a far cry from the Halloween parties and haunted houses they'd been frequenting, but there was something about it that felt perfect. It was simple, easy, and exactly what they needed.

"Soup's ready!" Tom called, making his way into the living room.

Ella turned, her face lighting up as she saw the tray of food. "Oh, that smells amazing! You've really outdone yourself."

Tom chuckled, setting the tray down on the coffee table. "It's just soup. But I'm glad it passes the test."

Ella grinned, settling onto the couch as she grabbed one of the bowls. "Pumpkin soup on Halloween? It's perfect."

Tom sat down beside her, taking his own bowl and leaning back against the cushions. The candles flickered softly around them, and the glow of the TV cast a warm light over the room. Outside, the sounds of Halloween—children laughing, leaves rustling, and the occasional doorbell—created a peaceful backdrop for their quiet night in.

"So," Tom said, glancing at the stack of movies on the table. "What's first on the list?"

Ella leaned forward, picking up the remote and flipping through the options. "I think we should start with *Hocus Pocus*. It's the ultimate Halloween classic."

Tom smiled, nodding. "Good choice."

As the opening credits of *Hocus Pocus* rolled across the screen, Ella snuggled closer to him, her head resting on his shoulder. The warmth of her body against his was comforting, and Tom felt a sense of peace settle over him. It was different from the excitement and thrill of their other Halloween adventures, but in a way, it was even better. There was something about this quiet, cozy night at home that felt intimate and special—like they were creating a new tradition just for the two of them.

Halfway through the movie, Tom glanced down at Ella, who was completely absorbed in the film. Her eyes sparkled with the same excitement he had seen on their first Halloween adventure together, and he couldn't help but smile. She had a way of making even the simplest moments feel magical, and Tom realized just how much he loved sharing these moments with her.

"Are you having fun?" Tom asked softly, his voice barely above a whisper.

Ella turned to him, her smile soft and genuine. "I'm having the best time," she said, her hand reaching for his. "This is exactly what I wanted—a quiet night with you."

Tom squeezed her hand, feeling his heart swell with affection. "Me too. It's nice to slow down for once."

They continued watching the movie, laughing at the antics of the Sanderson sisters and quoting their favorite lines from memory. The soup bowls were soon replaced with popcorn, and the cider was sipped slowly as they settled deeper into their cozy Halloween cocoon.

By the time *Hocus Pocus* ended, the sky outside had grown darker, and the trick-or-treaters had mostly disappeared. The apartment was quiet now, save for the faint hum of the wind outside and the crackle of the candles burning low on the counter.

Ella stretched, glancing at the stack of movies. "What's next? *The Nightmare Before Christmas?*"

Tom nodded, his smile widening. "Definitely. That's a must."

As the next movie began, Tom leaned back against the cushions, pulling the blanket over them both. Ella rested her head on his chest, her breathing soft and steady, and Tom felt a wave of contentment wash over him. This night—this simple, quiet Halloween night—was everything he hadn't realized he needed.

For the past few weeks, they had been caught up in the whirlwind of Halloween festivities—costume competitions, haunted houses, and thrilling adventures. But here, in the warmth of his apartment, with Ella beside him, Tom felt a deeper connection, a sense of home that had nothing to do with the excitement of the season and everything to do with the quiet moments they shared.

As the movie played, Tom found himself thinking about the future—about the Halloweens yet to come and the traditions they might build together. The thought of spending more nights like this, of creating new memories year after year, filled him with a quiet kind of happiness, the kind that settled deep in his chest and lingered there, warm and reassuring.

After *The Nightmare Before Christmas* ended, Ella sat up, stretching and yawning softly. "I love this," she said quietly, glancing around the room. "This night, this feeling—it's exactly what I imagined."

Tom smiled, sitting up beside her. "Yeah? You're not missing all the excitement of the parties and haunted houses?"

Ella shook her head, her smile soft. "Not at all. Don't get me wrong, all that stuff was amazing, but... this feels different. It feels like us, you know? Like our own little Halloween tradition."

Tom nodded, understanding exactly what she meant. "It does feel like that, doesn't it?"

Ella leaned in, resting her head on his shoulder again. "I think this should be our new tradition. Every year, we'll have a crazy, adventure-filled Halloween season, but on Halloween night, we'll stay in. Just us, just like this."

Tom smiled, wrapping his arm around her. "I love that idea. It sounds perfect."

They sat in comfortable silence for a while, watching the flames of the candles flicker and dance in the dim light. The quiet of the room, the warmth of their shared space, and the ease of their connection made the night feel almost magical, like they were creating something sacred between them—a space where they could just be, without the need for anything more than each other's company.

"I think this has been my favorite Halloween," Ella said softly, her voice barely above a whisper.

Tom pressed a kiss to the top of her head, feeling the truth of her words settle into his own heart. "Mine too."

Chapter 20: The Night of the Masquerade Ball

The evening of the masquerade ball had finally arrived, and Tom could feel a mix of excitement and nervousness bubbling inside him. The invitation had been sitting on his counter for weeks, its elegant script promising an unforgettable night of mystery, music, and glamour. He hadn't been to anything like this before, but Ella had been thrilled at the idea of attending a Halloween masquerade ball, and her excitement had rubbed off on him.

He stood in front of the mirror, adjusting the dark, intricately designed mask that covered half his face. The mask was made of black lace and satin, with silver accents that gleamed faintly in the dim light of his bedroom. It was striking, adding an air of mystery to his otherwise simple black suit. Tom had never considered himself someone who would wear a mask to an event, but tonight felt different—it felt like stepping into a different world.

As he finished adjusting his mask, there was a soft knock at the door. His heart skipped a beat, knowing it was Ella.

"Coming!" he called out, making his way to the door.

When he opened it, Tom's breath caught in his throat. Ella stood before him, dressed in an elegant, floor-length gown of deep emerald green, the fabric shimmering as she moved. Her mask matched her dress perfectly—ornate and delicate, with small gems woven into the design that sparkled under the hallway light. Her hair was swept up in loose waves, and the mask highlighted her eyes, making them look even more captivating than usual.

"You look... incredible," Tom said, his voice filled with awe.

Ella smiled, her cheeks flushing slightly beneath the mask. "So do you," she replied, her gaze sweeping over him appreciatively. "I knew you'd pull off the whole 'mysterious gentleman' look."

Tom laughed softly, stepping aside to let her in. "You definitely make the 'mysterious lady' look effortless."

Ella twirled playfully, letting the skirt of her dress swirl around her legs. "I've been looking forward to this night for weeks. I can't believe it's finally here."

Tom nodded, feeling the excitement build. The masquerade ball was being held at the town's historic ballroom, a grand building that was often used for weddings and formal events. But tonight, it had been transformed into something else entirely—something magical and a little bit eerie. The thought of walking into a room filled with masked strangers, all dressed to the nines, sent a thrill through him.

"Ready to go?" Tom asked, offering Ella his arm.

She smiled, taking his arm with a nod. "Let's do this."

The drive to the ballroom was filled with laughter and anticipation. As they approached the grand building, Tom could see the soft glow of lanterns lighting the pathway up to the entrance. A line of cars had already formed, and elegantly dressed guests were stepping out, their faces hidden behind intricate masks.

The ballroom itself was stunning. The entrance was framed by tall pillars wrapped in dark, shimmering fabric, and the air was thick with the scent of autumn flowers and burning candles. They stepped inside, and Tom felt as though they had entered another world. The grand hall was draped in rich, velvety curtains of black and deep red, while crystal chandeliers hung from the ceiling, casting a warm, flickering glow over the crowd.

Masked guests filled the room, their gowns and tuxedos creating a kaleidoscope of colors as they danced, mingled, and laughed. The music—soft and haunting—played from a small orchestra seated in the corner, adding to the dreamlike atmosphere of the evening.

"Wow," Ella whispered, her eyes wide as she took in the sight before them. "This is incredible."

Tom nodded, equally mesmerized by the setting. "It feels like we've stepped into a different time."

They made their way through the crowd, their masks allowing them to blend in seamlessly with the other guests. There was something thrilling about the anonymity of it all—knowing that no one could recognize them, that they were just two faces among a sea of strangers.

Ella's eyes sparkled as she looked around. "I love the mystery of this. It's like being part of a story—where anything can happen."

Tom smiled, understanding what she meant. There was a sense of possibility in the air, an energy that made the night feel alive with potential. He was used to the predictable, the familiar, but tonight felt different. Tonight, there were no rules, no expectations—just the magic of the masquerade.

As they moved through the room, a waiter approached, offering them flutes of champagne. Tom took two glasses, handing one to Ella. "To a night of mystery," he said with a grin, raising his glass.

Ella clinked her glass against his. "To a night we'll never forget."

They sipped their champagne as they wandered through the ballroom, stopping to admire the extravagant decorations. Dark roses and flickering candles adorned every table, and the chandeliers overhead sparkled like stars in the night sky. The crowd buzzed with excitement, their voices a low hum beneath the music, and everywhere Tom looked, he saw flashes of masked faces, each one as enigmatic as the next.

After a while, Ella's eyes brightened as she spotted the dance floor, where couples were moving in graceful steps to the soft music. "Do you want to dance?" she asked, her voice hopeful.

Tom hesitated for a moment. He wasn't much of a dancer, but the look in Ella's eyes made him want to try. "I'm not great at it, but... yeah, let's dance."

Ella grinned, taking his hand and leading him toward the dance floor. The music was slow and melodic, and as they joined the other couples, Tom felt a slight nervousness creep in. But Ella's hand in his, warm and steady, calmed him. They began to move together, swaying gently to the rhythm, and Tom found that it wasn't nearly as difficult as he'd imagined.

"You're doing great," Ella whispered, her voice teasing.

Tom chuckled, his nerves easing. "You make it easy."

They continued to dance, their movements growing more fluid with each passing moment. The room seemed to fade away, the other dancers blurring into the background as Tom focused on Ella—the way her eyes sparkled beneath her mask, the soft smile on her lips, the way her dress moved as they spun together.

For the first time in weeks, Tom felt completely at peace. It wasn't the thrill of a haunted house or the excitement of a costume contest. It was something quieter, deeper. He felt connected to Ella in a way that went beyond the fun they'd been having all month. This moment, this dance, was something special.

As the song came to an end, they slowed to a stop, their gazes locking beneath their masks. For a moment, neither of them spoke, the magic of the masquerade wrapping around them like a soft embrace.

"Thank you for tonight," Ella whispered, her voice filled with emotion. "This has been... perfect."

Tom smiled, leaning in closer. "I think this might be my favorite night yet."

Chapter 21: The Unexpected Twist

The morning after the masquerade ball, Tom woke up feeling unusually energized. The night had been magical—one of those rare, perfect moments when everything seemed to align. Dancing with Ella, the mystery of the masks, and the laughter shared had left him in a state of quiet contentment.

As he lay in bed, replaying the night's events in his mind, his phone buzzed with a message from Ella.

Ella: "Morning, mystery man. Last night was incredible. 😏 But I have a surprise for you... Meet me at the park by 2 PM. Trust me, it'll be fun. 💀🎃"

Tom smiled, his curiosity piqued. Ella always had something up her sleeve, and after weeks of Halloween adventures together, he'd learned that her surprises were always a mix of fun and excitement. But there was something about the skull and pumpkin emojis that made him wonder if this time, it might be more than just another casual outing.

He quickly replied, agreeing to meet her at the park, then spent the rest of the morning wondering what she had planned. Hadn't they already done everything on their Halloween adventure list? The masquerade ball felt like the perfect grand finale—what could possibly be next?

By the time 2 PM rolled around, Tom was at the park, sitting on a bench near the entrance. The air was crisp, filled with the familiar scents of autumn leaves and the last remnants of Halloween excitement. Kids were still running around in their costumes, clutching bags of candy, while parents strolled leisurely behind them.

Tom spotted Ella in the distance, walking toward him with a mischievous smile on her face. She looked casual but effortlessly beautiful in a deep maroon sweater, her hair loosely tied back, and her eyes gleaming with excitement. But what caught Tom's attention most was the small, crumpled piece of paper she held in her hand.

"You're here," Ella said, plopping down beside him on the bench, her breath slightly visible in the cool air. "Ready for your surprise?"

Tom grinned. "I've been thinking about it all morning. What are we doing?"

Ella leaned in closer, handing him the piece of paper. "It's a scavenger hunt. But not just any scavenger hunt—a haunted one."

Tom raised an eyebrow, unfolding the paper. "A haunted scavenger hunt? Isn't that a little late? Halloween was yesterday."

Ella's eyes twinkled as she leaned back against the bench, crossing her arms with a satisfied grin. "That's the twist. The scavenger hunt started last night, after the masquerade ball. It's been going on since midnight, and we're the final participants."

Tom looked down at the paper, scanning the list of clues written in Ella's neat handwriting. It was a series of cryptic hints, each one leading to a different location around town. There were six clues in total, and the final one was marked with a question mark—an unknown destination that piqued his curiosity.

Tom looked up at her, his heart racing with a mix of excitement and intrigue. "So, what happens when we finish?"

Ella shrugged, her smile widening. "That's for me to know and you to find out."

Tom couldn't help but laugh. "Of course it is."

He stood up, folding the paper and tucking it into his jacket pocket. "Alright, let's get started. What's the first clue?"

Ella jumped up, pulling the paper out and reading the first line aloud: "*In the place where the old swings creak, a secret awaits for those who seek.*"

Tom thought for a moment, picturing the old swing set at the far end of the park. It had been there for decades, its wooden beams weathered by years of use. The swings were rarely used anymore, but their eerie creaking sound was something of a local legend, especially on windy nights.

"The old swing set," Tom said, pointing toward the far side of the park.

Ella nodded, her excitement growing. "Let's go."

They made their way across the park, the leaves crunching underfoot as they followed the path that wound through the trees. The swing set came into view, its rusty chains swaying gently in the breeze, and Tom felt a strange sense of nostalgia as they approached. He hadn't been to this part of the park in years.

Ella motioned for him to check under the swings. "There's supposed to be something hidden here."

Tom crouched down, searching the ground beneath the swings until his fingers brushed against something cold and metallic. He pulled it out—a small key, old and tarnished, with an intricate design etched into the handle.

Ella grinned, her eyes lighting up. "That's it! You found the key."

Tom stood up, holding the key in his hand. "Okay, now what?"

Ella unfolded the paper again, reading the next clue: "*The key you've found will unlock a door, where secrets lie behind folklore. The place you seek is tall and old, where stories of spirits are often told.*"

Tom thought for a moment, running through the possible locations in his mind. "Tall and old, with stories of spirits... The library?"

Ella nodded. "Exactly. The library's been around forever, and people always say it's haunted."

The library was one of the oldest buildings in town, with towering bookshelves and creaky floors that had hosted generations of readers. It was the perfect setting for the next stop in their haunted scavenger hunt.

As they made their way to the library, Tom's excitement grew. He had always loved scavenger hunts as a kid, and now, with Ella by his side, this one felt even more thrilling. There was something mysterious and enchanting about the whole thing—the clues, the hidden key, and the sense that they were being drawn into a larger story.

When they reached the library, the old stone building stood quietly in the late afternoon light, its arched windows glowing faintly from the setting sun. The door creaked as they entered, and Tom could feel the cool, musty air inside.

Ella led the way to the back of the library, where a small, seldom-used reading room sat tucked away behind the stacks. It was one of the quieter spots in the building, and as they stepped inside, Tom noticed something unusual. On the far side of the room, an old wooden chest sat on the floor, slightly ajar.

Tom's pulse quickened as he crossed the room. "Is this part of it?"

Ella smiled knowingly. "Why don't you open it and find out?"

Tom pulled the lid open carefully, revealing a small black envelope inside. He picked it up, feeling the weight of it in his hands, and turned it over. His name was written on the front in elegant, silver script.

"What's this?" Tom asked, looking up at Ella, who was watching him with a mix of excitement and nervousness.

"Open it," she said softly.

Tom did as she asked, sliding the envelope open and pulling out a folded piece of paper. His heart raced as he unfolded it, his eyes scanning the message inside:

Tom,

You've made every moment of this Halloween season unforgettable. And as much as I love the fun and games, there's something I need to tell you. This isn't just a scavenger hunt—it's my way of saying that I've fallen for you. Completely. This season, this adventure, has made me realize that I want more than just a Halloween fling. I want to see what's next for us.

If you feel the same, meet me outside at the last stop—the place where it all began.

Tom's breath caught in his throat as he looked up at Ella, her eyes filled with hope. His mind raced back to the beginning of their

Halloween adventure—to the first time they had met while picking out Halloween decorations. The store, the moment, the spark—it had all started there.

    Ella smiled nervously. "So... what do you think?"

    Tom didn't need a second to think. "I think... I'm meeting you outside."

Chapter 22: Halloween Morning Fun

It was Halloween morning, and for the first time in years, Tom felt an overwhelming sense of excitement—not the kind that came from haunted houses or elaborate costumes, but the quiet thrill of waking up next to someone who had changed his life in more ways than he ever could have imagined.

He glanced over at Ella, who was still fast asleep, her face peaceful and calm as the morning light brushed against her skin. Her hair was slightly messy from sleep, but to Tom, she had never looked more beautiful. Last night had been unforgettable—the scavenger hunt, the confession in the library, the way everything had come together in a moment that felt like it had been written just for them.

Tom smiled to himself, thinking about how far they had come in such a short time. What had started as a chance encounter while picking out Halloween decorations had grown into something deeper, something real. And now, waking up next to Ella, he knew this Halloween would be different. It would be a celebration, not just of the holiday, but of the connection they had built and the future they were about to create together.

He carefully slid out of bed, trying not to wake her, and headed to the kitchen. The apartment was still quiet, the kind of peaceful stillness that came with early morning. Tom had an idea—something small, but meaningful—that would make their Halloween morning even more special.

Ella had told him about the traditions she used to share with her mom growing up, and one of them stood out in his mind: a Halloween breakfast. Ghost-shaped pancakes, pumpkin muffins, and warm cider had always marked the start of her Halloween mornings as a kid, and Tom thought it would be the perfect way to surprise her today.

He started by mixing up a batch of pancake batter, carefully adding orange food coloring to give the pancakes a pumpkin-like hue. He found a ghost-shaped cookie cutter in one of the drawers—a remnant of their recent Halloween baking adventures—and used it to shape the pancakes as they cooked on the griddle. The apartment soon filled with the sweet smell of batter and cinnamon, the warmth of the stove creating a cozy atmosphere.

As he worked, Tom could hear the faint sounds of Ella stirring in the bedroom. He wanted everything to be ready by the time she woke up, so he quickly set the table, placing the ghost-shaped pancakes on plates along with small pumpkin muffins he had bought the day before. He poured two mugs of warm apple cider, the steam rising from the mugs in soft curls.

Just as he was finishing, Ella appeared in the doorway, wrapped in a blanket and rubbing her eyes sleepily. She blinked at the sight before her, a look of surprise and joy spreading across her face.

"Good morning," Tom said, his voice warm as he motioned toward the table. "I figured I'd bring a little Halloween tradition to our morning."

Ella's eyes widened as she took in the ghost-shaped pancakes and the rest of the Halloween-themed breakfast. She smiled, her heart clearly touched by the gesture. "You did all this?"

Tom nodded, smiling as he set down the cider mugs. "I remember you told me about the breakfasts you used to have with your mom. I thought it'd be fun to bring that back for us."

Ella walked over, her eyes shining as she wrapped her arms around him in a tight hug. "You're amazing. This is perfect."

Tom hugged her back, feeling the warmth of her embrace. "I'm just glad I didn't burn the pancakes."

Ella laughed, pulling back slightly to look at the table again. "You even got the ghost shapes right! I'm impressed."

They sat down at the table, their plates filled with pancakes and muffins, the sweet smell of cinnamon and apple filling the room. Tom watched as Ella took her first bite of the pancakes, her smile widening as she chewed.

"These are delicious," she said between bites. "You really nailed it."

Tom grinned, feeling a sense of pride. "I had a pretty good motivator."

They ate together in comfortable silence for a while, the soft morning light filtering through the windows. Outside, the town was slowly waking up to Halloween, and Tom could hear the faint sounds of kids already starting to plan their trick-or-treat routes. It was a day filled with excitement and anticipation, but for Tom and Ella, this quiet morning felt like the perfect way to start the festivities.

As they finished breakfast, Ella leaned back in her chair, her eyes sparkling with contentment. "This has been the best Halloween season of my life," she said softly. "I don't think anything can top it."

Tom smiled, reaching across the table to take her hand. "I think we've set a pretty high bar. But I have a feeling we'll find ways to keep topping it."

Ella laughed, nodding in agreement. "I think you're right."

They spent the rest of the morning lounging in the living room, sipping cider and watching classic Halloween cartoons that Tom had dug out of his movie collection. It was the perfect mix of nostalgia and relaxation, the kind of Halloween morning that didn't require costumes or haunted houses to feel special. It was the small things—the shared laughter, the warmth of the cider, and the quiet moments together—that made it meaningful.

At one point, Ella leaned her head on Tom's shoulder, her voice soft. "I love that we've made so many new traditions this year. But this... just us, here... this feels like the one I'll remember most."

Tom smiled, resting his head against hers. "Me too. It's been incredible—everything we've done. But I think this morning... this is the kind of Halloween tradition I want to keep."

Ella turned to look at him, her eyes filled with warmth. "So, what's the plan for the rest of the day?"

Tom thought for a moment, then grinned. "Well, we've got the pumpkin soup in the fridge, and we still have plenty of candy left from our scavenger hunt. I say we have a cozy afternoon in, watch more movies, and then head out for a walk later. We can see all the trick-or-treaters in their costumes."

Ella's smile widened. "That sounds perfect."

Chapter 23: Halloween Proposal

Tom and Ella had spent the afternoon lounging at home, watching Halloween classics and soaking up the last few hours of quiet before the evening's festivities began. But Tom had a different plan for how this Halloween night would unfold—something far more significant than just trick-or-treating or watching movies. He had been planning this moment for weeks, and tonight, he knew, would change everything.

As they finished watching yet another Halloween movie, Ella stretched out on the couch, smiling contentedly. "This has been the best Halloween," she said softly. "I don't want it to end."

Tom's heart pounded in his chest as he listened to her, knowing that what he was about to do would make this Halloween one they would never forget. He had been carrying the small, velvet box in his jacket pocket all day, waiting for the perfect moment to ask her the question that had been on his mind since the Halloween season had begun.

He wanted the proposal to be meaningful, something that reflected all the incredible moments they had shared over the past month. Halloween had brought them together, and now, it felt like the right time to take the next step. Ella had become more than just his partner in Halloween adventures—she had become his everything.

"Hey," Tom said softly, standing up and holding out his hand. "How about we take a walk before the trick-or-treaters really start flooding the streets? It's the perfect time—right before dusk."

Ella looked up at him, smiling as she took his hand. "That sounds great. It's beautiful outside."

Tom helped her up, his heart still racing as he tried to keep his nerves in check. They grabbed their jackets and stepped out into the cool evening air, the sounds of Halloween all around them—kids laughing, leaves crunching beneath their feet, and the faint hum of spooky music coming from nearby houses.

They walked down the familiar streets, passing by homes decorated with jack-o'-lanterns, cobwebs, and ghostly figures. The air was filled with the scent of caramel apples and wood smoke from chimneys, and the sky overhead was painted in shades of purple and orange as the sun set behind the trees.

As they walked, Tom kept his hand in his pocket, his fingers brushing against the small velvet box. He was waiting for the right moment—the moment when everything would fall into place.

They made their way toward the park, where the old swing set stood, the same one where they had started the haunted scavenger hunt just the day before. The park was quieter now, with only a few families walking along the paths, their children dressed in costumes and eagerly anticipating the night ahead.

Tom led Ella toward the swings, and they sat down side by side, watching the last of the daylight fade into twilight. The park was bathed in a soft glow from the streetlamps, and for a moment, everything felt still, as if the world had paused just for them.

"This place brings back memories," Ella said with a smile, her eyes reflecting the golden light. "Our scavenger hunt. That was one of the best surprises ever."

Tom smiled, his heart pounding in his chest. "Yeah, it was. But I think tonight's going to be even more memorable."

Ella tilted her head, curiosity flickering in her eyes. "Oh? Do you have another surprise planned?"

Tom took a deep breath, trying to steady himself as he turned to face her. His hand slipped out of his pocket, and before he could second-guess himself, he pulled out the small velvet box.

Ella's eyes widened in surprise, her hand instinctively flying to her mouth as she realized what was happening. Tom could see the emotions swirling in her eyes—shock, excitement, and something deeper, something that made his heart swell with love.

"Ella," Tom began, his voice soft but steady, "I've spent the last few weeks having the best time of my life with you. This Halloween season has been amazing—not because of the decorations, or the costumes, or even the haunted houses. It's been amazing because of you."

Ella's eyes filled with tears as she listened, her hand still covering her mouth as she watched him, her expression filled with emotion.

"I've realized something over the past few weeks," Tom continued, his voice growing more confident. "I don't want this to be just a Halloween thing, or a seasonal adventure. I want this—us—to be forever. You've made me happier than I've ever been, and I want to spend the rest of my life making you as happy as you've made me."

With that, Tom knelt down on one knee, holding up the small velvet box. He opened it, revealing a beautiful, simple diamond ring that sparkled in the fading light.

"Ella," Tom said, his heart in his throat, "will you marry me?"

For a moment, everything seemed to stand still. The sounds of Halloween—the laughter, the wind, the rustling leaves—all faded into the background as Tom waited, his heart pounding with anticipation.

Ella's eyes filled with tears as she nodded, her voice barely above a whisper. "Yes," she said, her voice breaking with emotion. "Yes, Tom, I'll marry you."

Tom's heart soared as he stood up, slipping the ring onto her finger. The moment their hands touched, it felt as though everything had clicked into place. This was it—this was their forever.

Ella threw her arms around him, hugging him tightly as tears of happiness streamed down her face. "I can't believe it," she whispered, her voice filled with awe. "This is the best Halloween ever."

Tom laughed, holding her close as he whispered in her ear. "I wanted to make sure this Halloween was one we'd never forget."

They stood there for a long time, wrapped in each other's arms as the night grew darker around them. The world seemed to disappear, leaving only the two of them in the quiet, magical space they had created together.

As they finally pulled away, Ella looked down at the ring on her finger, her eyes shining with joy. "I love you, Tom," she whispered, her voice soft and filled with emotion.

Tom smiled, his heart full. "I love you too, Ella. More than anything."

They walked back toward the streets, hand in hand, the sounds of Halloween night filling the air once again. But this time, everything felt different. They weren't just Tom and Ella, two people who had met by chance in a store full of Halloween decorations. They were something more now—something lasting.

Chapter 24: A Halloween Wedding Dream

The days after Tom's Halloween proposal felt like a whirlwind of excitement and joy. Ella could hardly believe it had all happened—the perfect scavenger hunt, the heartfelt confession, and the moment when Tom had knelt before her with that beautiful ring. It felt like a dream she never wanted to wake up from, and now, as they sat together on the couch, wedding plans already swirling in their minds, Ella found herself lost in the thought of what their wedding day might look like.

She glanced at Tom, who was scrolling through his phone, looking at potential venues for their big day. He was as enthusiastic as ever, determined to find a way to make their wedding just as special as the Halloween adventures they had shared.

"I can't believe we're already talking about the wedding," Ella said, her voice filled with wonder. "It feels like just yesterday we were dressing up for that Halloween party."

Tom smiled, setting his phone down and turning to face her. "It does feel fast, but I think we both know this is right. And besides, it's exciting to plan the rest of our lives together."

Ella nodded, her heart swelling at his words. She had never been one to dream of a traditional wedding, but with Tom, the idea of a celebration—one that reflected who they were as a couple—felt like something she genuinely wanted.

"Okay," Ella said, sitting up a little straighter. "So, what if we did something really different? What if we made our wedding a Halloween wedding?"

Tom raised an eyebrow, clearly intrigued. "A Halloween wedding? You mean… themed?"

Ella nodded, her eyes sparkling as the idea started to take shape in her mind. "Yeah! I mean, Halloween brought us together. It's been such a huge part of our story, and I think it could be fun to incorporate some of that magic into our wedding."

Tom smiled, clearly warming up to the idea. "You know, I actually love that. It would be unique, and it would really represent us."

Ella's mind raced as she imagined what their Halloween-themed wedding might look like. She could picture the fall colors—rich oranges, deep purples, and hints of black woven into the décor. The tables could be decorated with pumpkins and flickering candles, and the whole venue could be transformed into a whimsical, spooky setting, filled with the enchantment of the holiday they both loved.

"Think about it," Ella said, her excitement growing. "We could have a masquerade ball theme, where everyone wears masks. We could serve pumpkin-flavored everything—pumpkin soup, pumpkin pies—and instead of a traditional cake, we could have a spooky, haunted wedding cake."

Tom's grin widened as he listened, clearly getting more excited by the minute. "And the venue could be a historic place, somewhere with a lot of character. Maybe an old mansion or a beautiful, rustic barn. Something that gives off that old, haunted vibe but still feels elegant."

Ella nodded enthusiastically. "Exactly! It would be fun, but still romantic. And we could have all these little Halloween touches, like carved pumpkins lining the aisle, or maybe even some kind of Halloween-themed favors for the guests."

Tom laughed, his eyes lighting up as he imagined the scene. "I can see it now—a Halloween wedding that people will be talking about for years."

They spent the next hour brainstorming ideas for their dream wedding, and with each new detail, the excitement grew. The idea of a Halloween wedding wasn't just fun—it felt right. It felt like a natural extension of who they were, of the connection they had built through their shared love of the holiday. Every decision seemed to come easily as they envisioned a day that would be filled with laughter, love, and just the right amount of Halloween magic.

At some point, Tom leaned back against the couch, his smile softening as he looked at Ella. "You know, I never really pictured what my wedding would be like before. I never thought about the details or how it would all come together. But now, sitting here with you, it feels like we're building something amazing together."

Ella reached for his hand, squeezing it gently. "I feel the same way. I didn't know what I wanted either, but now that we're talking about it… this feels perfect."

They sat there for a moment, their hands intertwined, as the glow of the candles in the living room flickered softly around them. Ella's mind wandered, picturing the ceremony itself—the two of them standing together in front of their friends and family, dressed in their wedding attire with a hint of Halloween flair.

The thought of wearing a wedding dress—a gorgeous gown with subtle Halloween accents, like lace detailing shaped like cobwebs or a flowing veil edged with dark fall leaves—made Ella smile. She could imagine herself walking down the aisle to the sound of soft, eerie music, the room filled with warm candlelight and the scent of pumpkin spice.

And Tom, standing at the altar, would be there waiting for her in a suit that matched the theme—classic but with a touch of something whimsical. Maybe he'd even wear a small mask for part of the ceremony, adding to the air of mystery and fun that surrounded the day.

"I think it's going to be beautiful," Ella said quietly, her voice filled with emotion. "Not just because of the theme, but because it's us. It's everything we've been through, everything we've shared."

Tom smiled, nodding as he held her hand a little tighter. "I can't wait to marry you, Ella."

Her heart swelled at his words, and for a moment, she felt overwhelmed by how much she loved him. This man—this incredible, thoughtful, loving man—had turned her world upside down in the best way possible. He had made her believe in love again, in the idea of a future filled with laughter and adventure.

"I can't wait to marry you too," Ella whispered, her voice thick with emotion.

They sat in comfortable silence for a few minutes, lost in their own thoughts about the future. The idea of a Halloween wedding had taken root, and Ella could already picture every detail—the soft glow of candles, the laughter of their friends and family, the way Tom would look at her when she walked down the aisle. It would be a celebration of their love, of their shared story, and of the holiday that had brought them together.

And as the evening wore on, Ella realized that this dream—this beautiful, enchanting Halloween wedding—wasn't just a fantasy. It was something they could make happen, something that would bring together the magic of Halloween and the love they shared in a way that was uniquely theirs.

"Do you think we'll actually do it?" Ella asked softly, her voice filled with hope.

Tom smiled, leaning in to kiss her gently on the forehead. "I think we can make anything happen. This is our story, and we get to write it however we want."

Chapter 25: The Relationship Vow

It had been weeks since Tom's Halloween proposal, and their lives had been a whirlwind of excitement and planning. The idea of a Halloween wedding had taken shape, and they had begun preparing for the ceremony, dreaming up all the details that would make their day as magical and unique as the love they shared. But today wasn't about the wedding. Today was about something even more important—something deeper.

Today was about the vow they were making to each other, a promise that went beyond rings or wedding plans. It was a vow of commitment, of love, and of forever.

Tom squeezed Ella's hand gently as they stood together in the quiet, secluded spot they had chosen for this moment. The trees around them rustled softly in the breeze, their leaves turning brilliant shades of orange and red, a final burst of color before winter set in.

"I can't believe we're here," Ella said softly, her voice filled with emotion. "It feels like everything we've been through has led us to this moment."

Tom smiled, his heart swelling with love as he looked at her. "I know. It feels like the perfect place for this."

They had chosen this hill for a reason—it was the spot where they had first gone pumpkin picking together, back at the start of their Halloween adventures. It was where their love had begun to take root, where the first sparks of something deeper had started to grow. And now, standing here again, it felt like the right place to make the promises that would shape their future.

Tom reached into his pocket and pulled out a small piece of paper, the edges slightly crumpled from being folded and unfolded so many times. He had written his vow to Ella in the quiet moments leading up to this day, carefully choosing the words that would express how much she meant to him.

"I wanted to say something," Tom began, his voice steady but filled with emotion. "Something that feels right for us."

Ella smiled softly, her eyes bright with unshed tears as she nodded for him to continue.

Tom took a deep breath, unfolding the paper. "Ella, from the moment we met, I knew there was something special about you. It wasn't just the way you lit up when you talked about Halloween or the way you made me laugh. It was the way you made me feel like I could be myself—like I didn't have to pretend to be anyone other than who I really am."

He paused, his gaze never leaving hers. "You've brought so much joy into my life, and I can't imagine a future without you. Every day with you has been an adventure, and I know that no matter what comes next, we'll face it together. You're my partner, my best friend, and the person I want to grow old with. I promise to love you with all that I am, to stand by you in every season, and to build a life with you that's filled with love, laughter, and a little bit of Halloween magic."

Ella's tears spilled over as she listened, her heart full. She hadn't expected Tom's words to move her so deeply, but they did. His sincerity, his love for her—it was everything she had ever dreamed of, and more.

Tom folded the paper and put it back in his pocket, smiling as he reached for her hand again. "Your turn," he said softly.

Ella took a deep breath, wiping her tears away as she gathered her thoughts. She hadn't written anything down, but the words were in her heart, ready to be spoken.

"Tom," she began, her voice trembling slightly, "you've made me believe in love again—in the kind of love that's real, that lasts. When we met, I didn't know what to expect. I didn't know that picking out Halloween decorations could lead to something so much more. But it did, and now I can't imagine my life without you."

She paused, her hand tightening around his. "You've shown me what it means to be loved, truly and deeply, and I promise to love you just as deeply in return. I promise to be by your side through every challenge and every joy. To build a life with you that's filled with adventure, with kindness, and with the kind of love that never fades."

Her voice caught as she continued, her eyes locking with his. "You're my home, Tom. Wherever we go, whatever we do, as long as we're together, I know we'll be okay."

Tom's throat tightened with emotion, his heart pounding as he listened to her words. He could feel the weight of the moment—the significance of what they were promising each other.

They stood there for a long time in silence, their hands clasped, the world around them quiet and still. This was more than just a vow—it was the foundation of everything that would come next. The wedding, the life they would build together, the moments they would share in the years to come—it all started here, with this promise.

"I love you," Tom said softly, his voice thick with emotion.

"I love you too," Ella whispered, her tears shining in the golden light of the setting sun.

And as the wind rustled through the trees, carrying with it the last whispers of autumn, Tom and Ella sealed their vow with a kiss—a kiss that held all the love, the hope, and the promise of their future together.

They stood there for a long time, wrapped in each other's arms, the world around them fading away. In that moment, it didn't matter what came next, what challenges they might face, or how their lives would change in the years to come. All that mattered was the love they had for each other, the connection that had brought them together, and the promise that they would face whatever came their way—together.

As the sun finally disappeared below the horizon, leaving the sky painted with the last hues of orange and purple, Tom and Ella walked hand in hand back toward the town, their hearts full. Halloween had brought them together, but it was their love—deep, steady, and unbreakable—that would carry them through every season that followed.

And as they made their way home, their relationship vow still fresh in their minds, they knew that this was just the beginning of their story—one filled with love, laughter, and a lifetime of new adventures.